# CONFESSIONS

## OF

## A SUCKER FOR

## LOVE

### STANLEY FRITZ

# CONFESSIONS

### OF A SUCKER FOR *Love*

# STANLEY FRITZ

Printed in the United States of America

First Printing, 2014

Keeping It Real Sports LLC

Artwork done by Brittany Campbell

ISBN 13:
978-0985286125
www.sucker4love.com
www.keepingitrealsports.com

*For Marilyn, Myke and Antie*

## Confessions Play list

Papa Roach- Last Resort
Linkin Park- The End
Eminem-Super Man
Jay Z- Big Pimpin
Eminem- Puke
My Chemical romance- Famous Last Words
Limp Bizkut- Behind Blue Eyes
Hoobastank- The Reason
Papa Roach- Hollywood whore
B.O.B.- Ghost in the Machine
B.O.B.- Lovelier than you
Eminem- Love The Way You Lie
My Chemical Romance- Mama
Papa Roach- Forever
Linkin Park- With You
Limp Bizkut- My way
112- missing you
Papa Roach- Scars
Eminem- No Love
Papa Roach- No more secrets
Hoobastank- Same Direction
Kanye West- Street Lights

Kanye West- Coldest Winter
John Legend- Used to love you
The Dream- Florida University
Maxwell- Fist Full Of Tears
D-12- Pimp Like Me
36 mafia- don't save her
Luther Vandross- Super Star
Billie Holliday- Strange Fruit
Sam Cook- Change gonna come
Stevie Wonder- Summer
Marilyn Manson- Sweet Dreams
Eminem- Love you more
Chris Brown- Right time to say good-bye
Papa Roach- Infest
Equinox- Call 911 Now!
Limp Bizkut- Break Stuff
Gorillas- Melancholy Hill

## Melancholy Hill

**Current Playlist:**

Gorillaz: Melancholy Hill

Hoobastank: Same Direction

Its 4:13am, and I'm sitting in front of this blank screen. If there is one thing that I know for sure, is this; I've gone through another bullshit relationship. I tried to lie to myself and say that I could change the outcome, but I think it was clear from the outset; she only wanted one thing and I obliged by being the same person that I have always been. And in the end I am right where I have ended up on so many occasions.

## I Suck At Girls

My history with women has not been the greatest. I've had bad luck with them for as long as I can remember and I don't even think the midwife who helped my mother deliver thought I was cute. Sometimes they love me, sometimes they hate me, but either way I don't seem to come out of this as the winner of many or any girl's hearts. So I've decided to write this book, and give you a taste of what its like to live this life. It's the life of every so-called "good guy". The ones you see holding the girls bag while she's flirting with the dick she met at the bar. I'm talking about the guy who waits for his girl because she does not want to have sex until she's married, and unbeknownst to him she's cheating on him with every other penis in sight, while he quietly masturbates in solitude. Yup those guys.

We make thousand dollar investments on Christmas gifts only to get a kiss on the cheek and an expired Game Stop gift card signed

"For Billy". My name is Eric. Yes we absolutely exist, this is the guy who sits and listens while his "BFF" complains that there are no good guys around. Sometimes he's no sucker; he's not a pushover. Instead he is the average guy. And in this average life of his he loses out on one girl or another because he's just too... Well average. This book is for us. For me, and you. My theory is that maybe if I reflect on every failed relationship, I can finally pinpoint the error of my ways and stop making the same mistakes. It's a noble thought at the least. And if all else fails, well fuck it, I tried. But in order for this to work, I need to start with high school, and the girl that started the trend...

## The Letter

It was the year 2003 that was a pretty muddled but interesting time for me. My life has always been dominated by music. I was still wildly obsessed with Eminem's third album, "The Eminem Show", as well as an avid listener of Papa Roach, Hoobastank, and Linkin Park. These artists "spoke to my soul" as many troubled teenagers have declared to their parents. No they really did, and it was through their music that I found myself getting through some of the more awkward years of my life. I guess you could say the song that best depicts my emotion towards women was "The End" which is of course sung by Linkin Park. I really did try hard; my entire goal in  life was to get a girlfriend. I was so hell bent that little things like whether we were compatible or if she liked me didn't matter. The only thing that was important was that I get one. The semantics were of no importance as long as she was hot, and willing to date me. There were plenty of girls in my high school, but since I didn't have a lick of confidence it had to be someone who was pretty but no so pretty that I would lose all motor skills and blow my chance. There was Roxanne, a brown skin Jamaican with the personality traits that today tell me she may have been the first hipster that I have ever known. Then there was Simone: a sassy Dominican who was also on the girls swimming team. Roxanne was really cool, and may have actually given me a shot if I asked her. But like most normal people; I have a deep hatred for hipsters. If I get too close I break out into hives. Simone was really pretty, and she and I spent a lot of time flirting during practice but she lived in the Bronx, and there was no way I was traveling two hours from Brooklyn to see her all the time. This left me with one last choice. Door number three. Her name was Anita; a pretty but quiet Puerto Rican; she was 5'2 with olive skin and black medium length hair, curly eyelashes, and shy brown eyes. She was one of those girls who was cute at first glance, but if you really took out the time to admire her, you would quickly notice that she was flat out beautiful (fortunately for me most guys in High School were not doing this). Outside of what I already stated, I literally knew nothing else about Anita, but who needs details when you're dealing with love?! During lunch everyone would hang out in the front of the school by the trailers (yes we had trailers) and she and her three friends would always be next to trailer number three. That was their little universe so in order to engage her I would have to enter her world and make it through the cock blocking grips of her three best friends, all three of who I have totally forgotten until this point. No I kid, I remember one of them. Her name was Prissy. I approached Anita and her "girly task force".

I'll spare you the details, long story short I asked her to be my girlfriend and because I'm just that awesome she said yes. This was the beginning of what is possibly the most awkward relationship in my entire history of dating. You see, I always wanted a girlfriend, but when I actually had one I had no idea what the hell I was supposed to do with her.

Anita and I had a relationship that consisted of almost zero communication, and lots of awkward glances. I never had her phone number, we never kissed, we never had communication outside of lunchtime, and during those moments I would hang out with her and her friends while taking notes of things that she liked to do. Yes, you heard me correctly I took notes. For the duration of our relationship, I carried around a little red pad, black ball point pen and I would ask her questions about herself then as creepily as possible, scribble my answer on to the pad while breathing heavily. We're not together today so it is obvious that these soon became useless facts. I should have tried to get them put under the Snapple bottles. Anita and I carried on like this for three strong weeks and it was the kind of relationship any socially awkward high school junior would want. But like most things that make no sense this affair had to come to an end, which brings me to the main part of this story.

Stuff Anita Likes

1.  R.Kelly Ignition remix (she has good taste)

2. O-Town (I should sing for her during lunch)

3. Lil Kim: (Anita likes SEX, YESSSS)

4. Anita does not like Doggie Style

5. Anita smells like a clean train cart.

5.5  Eric and Anita Forever!

It was a sunny Friday afternoon, and like most days I was clueless and excited. It was the last class of the day, and I had a long three-day weekend ahead. When I think back on that moment I realize now that it was Trevin's fault. Trevin was one of my best friends in High School; he was also a certified sex addict and the star of the basketball team. He had all of the girls and all of the influence, so it was only right that I bragged to him about my girl.

I mean seriously, this is a guy who rarely heard the word no from the girls on campus. He had first dibs on every prime trim in our High School, but I had gotten to Anita first.

*"Bro, Anita is soooooo Zexy (Guy language for attractive) you guys missed out. "Where have you been?!"*

I went on like this for about twenty minutes while Trevin, the teacher (Our swim team Coach) and my classmates watched in interest, and then suddenly there was a knock at the door. Of all people that could have been there at that moment it was Prissy. She looked right in my direction and started talking;

*"Hey ugly, I got a note from Anita for you, but read it alone because she put some freaky stuff in there"*

I walked up to her took the note and responded as if reading this note in public would be the last thing I would ever want to do. If only she really knew me. This was going to be the ultimate confirmation of my awesomeness. I asked Trevin to do the honors;

Hey Trev, read this letter and let everyone see how bad Anita has it for me".

Trevin opened the letter, read it to his self, laughed out loud, and then read it for everyone else to hear. Here is what it said.

*Hey babe, I like you a lot. You're really cool and everything, but it really creeps me out how you write shit in your little "Stalker Book" and more importantly Mike is super cute and wants to be my boyfriend. So you and I have to break up. Don't feel bad, I had Preston put a picture of me in your locker so you would have something to remember me by. Ok Cool later!*

It took me a moment to realize what had just happened, and by then everyone in the class including the teacher were laughing their Asses off. I looked around, took a deep breath and walked right out of the classroom. I had no idea where I was going or what I wanted to do, but after a few minutes I came to and realized I was staring at my locker. There was something inside so I put in the combination and opened it up. Guess what I found? A picture of Anita and Michael doing

Hey babe, I like you a lot. You're really cool and everything, but it really creeps me out how you write shit in your little "Stalker Book" and more importantly Mike is super cute and wants to be my boyfriend. So you and I have to break up. Don't feel bad, I had Preston put a picture of me in your locker so you would have something to remember me by. Ok Cool later!

couples pose for me to enjoy, and it was at that moment that I realized my journey with women would not be an easy one. Welcome to my story.

# Love, Or Maybe Just Horny

**Current Playlist:**

Linkin Park: Pushing Me Away

Linkin Park: About to Break

Linkin Park: Crawling

112: Missing You

36 Mafia: Don't save her

A few years ago, I couldn't imagine being able to share some of the most intimate moments of my life with complete strangers. It may seem small to you, but I have a battle scar for every failed relationship, and while most have healed and cause no pain, there are always one or two that never go away. I don't care what kind of guy you are, we all have or will have a story about a first love, and a first heartbreak, it's inevitable. In this story I'll share with you both of my firsts.

# Clara

Clara, Clara, Clara. If you're expecting things to improve after what I went through with Anita, you're a fucking moron. This is still high school, and as you will see once you go deeper into this book, I don't make the same mistake twice, I make them 15-20 times. When it comes to women I'm a slow learner. But back to Clara, what do I remember about said girl? OH, ok here is the best description I can give you: Breast, Ass, Hips, Lips and the sexiest fucking Spanish accent a virgin 17 year old had ever heard. But the best part about her was that no one in school ever paid her any attention. It's like she was waiting for me the entire time. She and I always flirted, but after the Anita fiasco I needed retribution, and a friend told me she was always DTF (Down to fuck). Clara was very receptive to my conversation and subtle charm, so she would be a perfect person to move on with. Seducing her was actually quite easy. One day during lunch I walked into the cafeteria with my basketball jersey on (Yup, I was on Varsity Basketball!) Approached her and just told her that we were together now; no seriously that's exactly what I did.

*"Hey Clara, we go together now, so don't talk to any other guy like that cause you're my girl"*

*"Am I'm just supposed to accept this?!"*

*"Well yeah"*

*"Ok! Well you gotta act like my boyfriend then. I better not see you talking to none of these putas"*

*"What 'bitches do you speak of?'*

*"You know what I mean, now meet me in front of school when you're done with basketball practice".*

From there it was official. I gave her my Nokia phone (With no minutes on it) as a token to show that she was mine; she "lost" the phone before the week was over. I learned my lesson from Anita, if I was going to have a girlfriend, I would actually have to interact with her. Things were different with Clara; we talked every night on the phone, and hung out every day at lunch. She and her best friend would come watch me during basketball practice, and she showed up to almost all of the games. It was the first time that I had ever connected with a girl and didn't feel awkward. We lived in one of the most dangerous parts of Brooklyn and both had dreams of going to college, becoming lawyers, and moving to the country where things would be quiet and simpler. We made it through the rest of eleventh grade together, and then senior year arrived.

# Don't Save her

There is a song by the rap group 36 Mafia; the song is called "Don't save her". If at all possible look it up and listen to the chorus while you read the rest of this chapter. In the event that you can't do that, it's a song about not saving women who enjoy living the "fast life" or THOT Life, as the wise Juicy J would say.

Ok now, back to the story. Clara and I were great together, but she had a few issues, ok I'm lying she had A LOT OF ISSUES! I don't say this to bash her, it's just the truth to it. She suffered from clinical depression, and the doctors suspected she was Bi Polar. She and her mother lived together but she was at constant war with her father or as she called him "My fucking sperm donor". Along with this, she had a girlfriend who she broke up with but couldn't get over and wanted to make miserable, all while being anemic which meant she would become light headed and "nauseous" when it was time to go to any math or science class. I don't know how you other guys were raised, but my father drilled into my head the idea that a man, is supposed to provide and protect any woman in his life. I considered myself a man so I took on all of her drama and made it mine. I would leave class to keep her company in the nurses office when she felt light headed, let her cry on my shoulder in the school staircase when she felt weighed down by emotions she couldn't explain, and listened intently to her frustrations over a father who could never seem to get it together. All in all I tried to protect her from herself, and be the pillar of strength I thought she needed me to be. It was then she told me that her ex-girlfriend went to our school, and though this girl may be someone I knew, I wouldn't try to find out who it was, and I didn't. I would do anything to protect this girl and I think she knew that.

Clara was one of those girls who always needed a hero, the simplest task would turn into the ultimate challenge and she would go from readily able to being on the brink of a nervous breakdown. She fed my need to provide and protect from day one. I put that cape on and was ready for duty at all times.

Did I mention that we were not having sex, oh I didn't?! Not only were we not having sex, we weren't even kissing. On the list of things that we had done, hugging and "staring longingly into each others eyes" were the only things checked off of our sexual list. We didn't even talk about sex, well I didn't. Any chance she got she was telling me how important it was for us to "stay pure" and "not give in to our skin". Little did she know I was giving into my skin every night with a picture of my dream lover, Kelly Kapowski and a warm bottle of Keri lotion, but that's probably too much information for you "Sex Experts".

# Teenage Boys Know Nothing About Sex

When I was 17 it seemed like a good idea to get sex advice from my idiot peer friends. Since I didn't have many friends, I went to my old reliable buddy, Trevin. Trevin had always been a ladies man so his sex advice was always trustworthy. He was the one that taught my friends and I that having sex in a hot tub could prevent pregnancy. And sure, Trevin had three kids, and another one on the way, but I'm confident that his pull out method was still a hundred percent successful. My local sex expert was no fan of Clara, and he would let me know any chance he got. It was one of the rare occasions where I didn't take his advice.

*"Listen to me! Girls like Clara want someone to boss them around, and I bet any money that she's the filthiest girl around; you just need to command sex with your eyes. Your eyes have to blaze doggie style, not missionary position, you get me?"*

*"How the hell do I show doggie style with my eyes?"*

*"You have much to learn young grasshopper. Until you learn how to simulate sexual positions with simple eye contact, Clara will never have sex with you. You don't even know bro, I've had sex with her like three times already, and it all happened with a blink."*

*"WHAT, how does that even work? You can't have sex with someone by just looking at them! This plan makes no sense, why can't I just kiss her?"*

*"Who said anything about kissing her?! You let her boyfriend take care of that business."*

*"But she's my girlfriend, I can't do that!"*

*"Listen Eric, trust me when I tell you that Clara is NOT GIRLFRIEND Material. TRUST ME!"*

*"But I love her!"*

*"Ok, but don't be mad later, because I definitely warned you."*

*"You're crazy, she's a virgin."*

Clara WAS NOT A VIRGIN! But we'll get to that in a moment. Things were going well between us when one day she asked me to meet her in the cafeteria at four. When I got there she was already waiting. Before I could utter a single word, she grabbed my face and started to kiss me... WITH TONGUE!!! I was shocked for the first 11 seconds, but once that was over I returned the kiss with full force. We were going at it for at least ten minutes before she stopped and surprised me again.

*"I want to lose it to you!"*

*"To Me?! Right Now?!"*

*"No not here nasty, I want it to be special; my mom goes to work tomorrow at 12:00pm let's cut school and have sex on her bed. Here I made you lunch, I hope you enjoy it."*

*"OK!!"!*

I went home that night on cloud nine! I was going to lose my V-Card to the girl of my dreams, plus she knew how to cook. The hero sandwich she gave me was awesome, although it was a bit heavy on the mayonnaise. Things could get no better. The night took forever to drag on, all I could think of was SEX with CLARA. What if I wasn't big enough for her, what if I came too quick, what if she changed her mind, what if she got hit by a truck?! The following day I went directly to Trevin to share the news

*Trevin, I need to talk, come out.*

*What's going on Bro?*

*Clara and me finally kissed. We made out for 20 minutes in the cafeteria after school yesterday, we're gonna cut school and go to her house to have sex but I've never done it before; should I shave my pubes?!*

*Trevin's face went from shock, to shame, to shocked again, then he just kind of stared at me while shaking his head for a bit.*

*Didn't I tell you that Clara was no good?!*

*Yeah but that's my girl and you don't know her like I do.*

*What time did you guys make out?!*

*Why does that matter?*

*Just answer the question*

*Around 4:00, why is that so important?!*

*Trevin put his face in his hands and said a few words in Spanish that I'm sure were curses. When he was done he looked me in the eye and started talking.*

*I don't know how to tell you this but I guess I'll just say it. A bunch of us found Clara getting busy with the basketball team.*

*What?*

*We caught her and like nine guys going at it.*

.........

*Why, when, how does something like that even happen, were you there?*

*I was, but don't worry I didn't do anything with her, I only watched. I told you she was a Hoe! It happened yesterday at around 3:00*

*At like exactly 3:00?*

*Maybe a little later, man I don't remember. Who keeps track of what time they witness a gang bang?! I heard she did it for a hero sandwich, must of been one hell of a sandwich.*

*We tongue kissed at 4:00 yesterday. For the first time...*

I didn't bother to give him a chance to respond. We both know what this meant. There were only two things I wanted at that moment, a toothbrush, and an explanation from Clara. I ran to the store, bought a toothbrush, and toothpaste, and then proceeded to brush until my gums hurt. I eventually found my gang bang lover during lunch period. I pulled her aside and demanded answers.

*Did you cheat on me?*

*Why would you ask me that?*

*Answer the question! Did you?*

*Well since you want to know so bad, yes. Yes I did. And you didn't even thank me for the sandwich asshole!*

*You really did that? But you kissed me the same day, what's wrong with you?*

*You don't get it, I have to do this, and the devil wants me to go wrong so I have to show him that he does not affect me. That's why I slept with the Boys and Girls basketball team, and that's why we can never be.*

Clara walked out of my life that day. I remember watching her leave the building and trying to figure out how things had taken such a drastic turn. How did we go from extremely happy to me finding out she was sleeping with half the school? Afterwards, I sat in my room and stared at the ceiling going through the motions until 9:30 when my phone went off. It was my alarm, reminding me to call Clara, because she would be done with church and her cell phones "Free nights, and weekends" feature kicked in at 9. That's when reality hit me, and it did so like a ton of bricks. I wanted to call her, but there was nothing to say. I wanted to be upset but I didn't know why or what I had to be upset about. All I knew was that I had these feelings for a girl who did not have them for me. I wanted to talk to someone about it, but all of my friends had warned me against dating her, so they would have nothing to say but "I told you so". I had never cared about a girl so much, so the way I was feeling was new. It was an unending sadness that I tried to ignore, but the feeling just wouldn't go away. There was no outlet I could use for relief; I was alone with my thoughts.

# I suck at getting dumped

I suck at being dumped, well maybe not in the actual getting dumped process. When it comes to that, it must be fairly easy to dump me since so many women have done it.

Actually I've become so versed at being dumped that I can tell you about the special techniques that are used to get out of relationships. There are three styles in which have been used to dump me.

1. **The switch up:** This style is used when the dumper uses masterful reverse psychology to make you feel like the breakup was mutual at best, or all your fault if they're good at it. People who use this technique are very intelligent and start planting the seeds for a easy getaway well before the actual breakup happens. Ever wonder why things that were fine last week are now a problem today? It might just be your partner planting those seeds.

**2. The Rotation Dumper:** This style is one used by people who are used to being in relationships and the idea of not being in one is unheard of. When things start heading downhill for the two of you they will more than likely check out mentally and emotionally, but remain there physically. This only last until they find a suitable replacement. More often than not the replacement is right under your nose, or in your bed depending on what your work schedule looks like.

3. **The Glacier:** I've dealt with this type more than any other, which will either tell you something about me, or the people I date. If I had to rank breakups, this would be number one from the sheer cruelty of it alone. The Glacier has no feelings, feels no regret, they only exist and act. Assholes and dick bags use this tactic. It's very simple to do actually; the dumper simply cuts off all communication with their partner. Don't call, text, tweet, email, or look at them. When that partner tries to make contact they simply ignore them. It is up to the other person to figure out that they have been dumped. No explanation is offered,

no communication whatsoever. The Glacier is especially evil because it leaves you with no closure, no answers and probably she'll shocked if you thought that things were going well.  If the person is really a dick, they will respond to you once only to inform you that you're annoying and to leave them alone, so like the switch up dumpers they attempt to put the burden of fault on you. Real classy ain't it? I don't think it's too hard for you to see that I absolutely hate Glaciers, getting dumped sucks, but being made to feel like you're not even worth acknowledging by someone you cared deeply about is another level of torture that I can never justify putting someone through.

I'm sure you would imagine that I have come up with many coping techniques in order to move on from these past relationships. Well you would be wrong. My healing processes include pent up emotions, alcohol consumption, and brooding.

Sometimes I wish my love life were like an 80's movie. If it were, after every bad relationship I could go on a walk along the beach with a tall glass of bourbon to reflect quietly while a dark and gritty song played, along with a montage of the relationship. When the song finished, I would be ready to move on with my life and never think about that girl again. Unfortunately, that's not how life works, not even in books.

# Moment of Honesty.

Remember when I said I would tell you how it really was? Oh, I didn't say that?! Whatever, I meant to so just listen. I have no idea how to process pain. A broken leg or gunshot wound is pretty simple to handle. You throw some spit or dirt in it and keep moving. But a broken heart is completely different. You will soon notice that this is a recurring theme in this book. I've been hearing this my entire life; we're supposed to be the non-feeling gentlemen of the world. But when I'm going through a bad breakup, all I can do is feel and have no idea what to do.

You can't talk to your guy friends about it, if you tell another woman it's more than likely that you're in the friend zone or she may lose respect for you. The only other options are alcohol, violence, or sleeping with any female that has a vagina.

Alcohol is expensive, violence is only awesome if you're kicking Cells ass in Dragon ball Z, and I can barely get one girl, so the idea of sleeping with multiple women was out of the question. That's how the mix tape came to life.

**The Mix Tape:**

Or you can call it my saving grace; after years of not knowing how to deal with all of my pent up emotions and feelings, I discovered the beautiful sound of music. This is not to give off the perception that I had never heard a single musical note. On the contrary, I listened to music everyday. It's just that I reached a point where I was now connecting to the songs on a completely different level. I was actually listening to the lyrics, and when that happened it was like. Light bulb clicked.

I discovered artists who could conceptualize all of the emotional turmoil that I dealt with on a three-minute track. I started putting together mix tapes to appease any mood I was in. I would compile all of my favorite songs into a single playlist then burn it onto a cd. When things were at their worse I could always drown my sorrows in a song, no matter what I was going through there was a song that could help me through it.

One of the hardest parts of getting through this heartbreak is that I did not really know how to deal with it. I remember being so angry; I would spend hours in my room listening to the Eminem show on repeat. "Superman was my favorite song. I wanted to be just like Eminem, he could turn his feelings off and only use women for sex. They didn't matter as people, he didn't care about their stories, and once he got what he wanted, he would be done with them. If only I could be as smooth as he was. There were days when I felt like a ticking time bomb. You can only sit in the dark with nothing but your bitter thoughts for so long before you start to feel something. It started off as a little fire at the pit of my stomach, slow and weak at first, but growing stronger and stronger every single day. It started off as something I would feel while alone, but eventually it carried over into my interaction with people and I noticed I was beginning to lash out at my friends. I would come home from school, go to my room, lock the door, and listen to that song on repeat. In my head, I would play a reel with all of my fondest memories with Clara. It was torture and therapy all at once. The memories hurt, but the song was able to say the things I either didn't know how, or was too scared to admit.

I slowly began to get out of my rut, and as my moods changed so did my musical selections. I became reflective and R Kelly's "Turn Back the Hands" became my go to song when I was trying to go through the past and figure out how we got here. But like all heartbreaks the pain and anger eventually fades away, the confusion is replaced with acceptance and in some cases we begin to resent the person that once meant so much to us. After months of being hurt and confused, I finally began to hate/resent Clara and Eamons "Don't Want You Back" was my anthem. I'll spare you the lyrics, but if you're really interested you should definitely download the song from ITunes. When all of these feelings had come and gone, the only thing I was left with was peace... or at least something like it. I was over the pain of being cheated on, I didn't miss Clara anymore, and she didn't invade my every thought. She did start a new trend though.. From that point on, there was always a song that would represent any major break up in my life. I had done it before but after Clara I would compile a soundtrack for every experience and woman to enter my life. As for the Clara saga, I had moved on and life seemed like it could finally progress. But that experience has had a long lasting effect on me. It's been almost ten years, and it never fails, whenever I hear that song "Missing You" from 112, I get a faint pain in my heart...

# The Friend Zone

**Current Playlist:**

Jimmy Eat World: Be Alright

Linkin Park: The End

Linkin Park: With You

For those of you who have no idea what I speak of when I mention the "friend zone," you will by the end of this passage.

The friend zone is a place that every man fears, every woman uses, and very few have ever escaped. By definition, it is the status that a woman gives to a man with whom she will never have sexual intercourse. However, this definition is not strong enough, as the friend zone goes so much deeper than that. Once you have been put into the friend zone, a woman will lean on you for emotional support, tell you about all of her problems, then show you erotic pictures of her and ask for advice on how to please other men in the bedroom. Nine out of ten times you are the exact kind of man that she should be pursuing a relationship with, but instead she decides to string you along, invite you over for movie nights, and make you watch chick flicks. By now, you have watched "The Notebook" more times than you care to admit, and it always ends with her saying; *"Why can't I find any good guys?"* This will likely inspire some kind of profanity-laced tirade under your breath but no worries, she won't hear. She's either too oblivious, or just doesn't care. When you are out in public, she latches on to your arm and purposely drives women away from you. Instead, she will fix you up with all of her fat friends with emotional baggage, because who doesn't want to date someone who will break into a crying fit because Tommy from the Power Rangers never responded to her love letter.

You will put in countless amounts of time and energy into her, leave your pride at the door on more occasions then you will care to remember, and just when it seems like she may finally see you for the great guy you are, some jerk will scoop her right away from your friendly embrace.

You're probably wondering how the hell you got here. What could I have done so wrong that caused her to cast me into the purgatory known as the *"friend zone?"* Here's the answer: You gave her what she wanted, and you did it too easily. Women want a bunch of things out of relationships, but most of all, they want emotional and spiritual support. They want that guy who will talk to them about their problems, and if they get into an argument, they want a guy who has no problem "crying it out." She wants the guy who's going to watch chick flicks with her without complaining, and then go running to the store to get her tampons and ice cream even though the New York Jets are playing. You made the mistake of giving this girl everything she ever wanted in a man. What you didn't know while doing this, is that while women may say they want all of those things, they are usually turned off by a guy that would literally do all of this stuff no questions asked. In response to your strange overtures, she must make a complete 180 from what she said she wanted and deny ever desiring a tool like you.

I've never understood how this works. I'll do everything I can to get the girl and still find a way to get shafted. Most guys I know demand at least three nude pictures before they would even make believe they cared how her day went. But you made the mistake of not only asking, but also listening while she spoke and then remembering little things. She appreciates this kind of behavior; and in her mind the only logical way to show you how much you mean to her is to never sleep with you. It should be clear by now that a simple man will never understand the inner workings of a woman's mind. That's just the way the Base God made things. But if you are in this sexless epidemic, fear not, because there are ways to break out of the friend zone.

There are a few ways you can choose to react upon the realization that you are in the friend zone. The first would be denial, but trust me; this is a painful road to travel. The second would be to quickly accept the terms of the friend zone status and have a one-sided mental relationship with her. Or three, you can choose to escape the friend zone. But when it comes to escaping there are only a few tactics that actually work. Some guys get frustrated and cut off all communication with the girl, but if she's done her job right, he will usually return soon after, most times even more broken than before. Others begin to talk about her friends and mention how attractive they are, but this may not always work, especially if they're fat or unattractive friends… If that's the case, she'll gladly fix you up with one of them. And the final one is a maneuver that is tricky no matter whom you try it on, but has been known to work. It's actually quite simple, just stop crying about her not wanting you and move on with your life. Hell, maybe she'll beg you to come back, probably not, but at least you'll have your dignity. If nothing else, maybe she'll feel really regretful and you can get to third base.

Let's take a step away from all of the superficial reasons I hate the "friend zone". Most guys will not admit this but somewhere deep down we have feelings and any guy who can at least acknowledge that he feels something will tell you that there are very few things worse than falling for someone who looks at you like a brother. It sucks to put in days, weeks, sometimes months worth of effort towards a girl who will only tell you, after an extended period of time, that she does not see your relationship with her going anywhere at all. I would gladly go through every bad break up all over again just to avoid the "friend zone". At least with the women who screwed you over, you had a chance. There are some women who will tell you that they had no idea what they were doing was wrong, and that they had no idea that the guy liked them. I seriously doubt that. Don't tell me that you didn't know this guy had feelings for you, or he waited until you already saw him as that to express his feelings. I'm not talking about those guys. They are what I like to call the dickless few. I'm talking about the guy who from day one let you know his intentions, takes you out or dates, calls you, and does all of the other things required to earn your trust. I bet you love what he's doing and it's exactly what you've been asking for. But for some reason it is not enough. Despite the chemistry you two share and the common interest and goals, you decides that his tactics are either "too good to be true" or, makes him "too nice" so you dump him with the famous line, "I really want you in my life as a friend". There are guys, who set themselves up for failure, but these guys clearly did all of the right things, so how do they end up on the losing side?

Speaking of stupid decisions and members of the dickless few, let me tell you of a time when I was a card holding member of that fraternity.

You ever met one of those girls who were like one of the guys, but hot, and with a vagina? Well I have. Her name was Monique and she was beautiful with a capital B. Okay, maybe I'm exaggerating, all I remember is that she had a huge ass, long black hair, full lips and loved to brag about how great at giving head she was. I would usually rebut by telling her that I was even better at getting it. We met through a mutual friend during a super bowl party; we'll call this friend Becky. Monique and I spent the entire game on the phone marveling at how much we hated Tom Brady and how bad we wanted the Panthers to win, they lost, but by the end of the conversation, I found out that she was on the basketball team, loved baseball, lived in Brooklyn, and was a Jets fan. Long story short, I was in love. We made plans to meet up that weekend, so I called Becky to share the good news. Becky was really pissed and let me have it. She went on and on about how I only liked girls who looked like they could be in pornos (but who doesn't?), and that Monique was going to hurt me. Then she started telling me that Monique was actually into girls, and had on several occasions hit on her. She clearly didn't know how to make a 17 year old virgin not like someone.

Like any wise man, I ignored Becky's warning and decided to go out with Monique anyway. In hindsight, our first date was really strange. We met at the entrance of Prospect Park, but didn't go inside. Instead we walked to the local McDonalds where I purchased a McFlurry that we shared. Then she asked me to race her to the train station, and bolted ahead, the train station was 15 blocks away from the McDonalds. Afterwards, I took her to this hole in the wall lounge in the village that I used to frequent. I loved it because they never carded, had top quality beer (Coors Light) and let me recite my shitty poetry. She ended up becoming really friendly with one of the regulars there named Shelly. Before I knew it, she would be at the lounge more than I was, and of course she was hanging out with Shelly. When Monique wasn't at the lounge with Shelly, she was at my house using my Internet and cooking weed brownies. We made out a few times, and I even got to third base, but she always got scared at the last minute. I wasn't even used to getting up to bat so this was more than enough to satisfy me. By week three of our relationship, I decided that Monique was the girl for me and decided to make her my girlfriend, and that's when things started to go straight to hell.

# Signs that a girl isn't into you

1.    **She Tells You:** Remember all of that talk about making Monique my girlfriend? Well she thought that this would be a great idea as well. There was only one small dilemma Monique was gay. Don't get me wrong; she's down to fool around with a guy from time to time if she thinks he's cute. But when it comes to being in an actual relationship, her heart could only go to a deserving woman. I knew this, and if for some reason I ever forgot, she was constantly reminding me. She and I would have long conversations about her desire for women, and why she could never connect with a man emotionally. Once after one of these discussions, she told me that I was just a pet spouse. Someone she could call her boyfriend but didn't have to commit to at all.

2.    **She's Always Talking About Other People:** When someone is in a relationship with you, it's probably a bad sign if they're always talking about the people they can't wait to have sex with. You should be especially

concerned if while on dates you have to hear about the sexual encounters your significant other has had with the "woman of her dreams", and if you are constantly giving her advice on how to deal with romantic issues not having to do with you, things are not going to work out. So yeah, Monique agreed to be my girlfriend, but that never stopped her from dating other women. In fact, she was developing a very strange attachment to Shelly. She blew me off multiple times to hang out with Shelly and would treat me like crap whenever the two of them got into arguments. I, of course, didn't take any of this into consideration. Lets be honest, who cares if your girlfriend doesn't like you? As long as she lets you tell all of your friends that the two of you are sleeping together and she buys you expensive snap backs.

3.     **She tells you she doesn't like you:** Well if the person you're dating tells you that they don't like you and you still stick around, you're just an idiot. Guess who the idiot was? After about a month of dating, Monique told me that she just wasn't into me, not

emotionally, not mentally and definitely not sexually, I chose to ignore this declaration and stick around.  Guess I shouldn't be too surprised about what happened next.

To celebrate our new relationship, I decided to dedicate a song for her at the next lounge open mic show. I professed my love for her on stage in front of a booming crowd of 15 people. Unfortunately, she was at the bar rounding third base with Shelly and never heard the dedication. I did a great job with the song, and got a standing ovation, but that's not really important when your fake girlfriend is making out with her real one.

# Hindsight is 20/20

Hindsight is stupid, I still believe the Friend Zone sucks, but I've learned a couple of things. I just thought I would share them with you.

1. **She Might be Making a Mistake, but it's hers to make-** I think what sucked the most about being told that I was only a friend, was that 8 out of 10 times that same girl would date a guy who she and I both knew would not give her what she wanted. More than likely, he would give her everything she didn't want and then some. But it was her choice to make; just because it makes sense for someone to be with you, doesn't mean that they should or have to. When you really care about someone and want them to be happy, you learn very quickly that there will be times that their decisions may not line up with what you think is right. But

you concede, because you respect them. Resenting someone you claim to care about for making a decision that you don't agree with is not only selfish, it's also the opposite of what someone does when they really have good intentions.

1. **Take a Look in The Mirror (Who Are You?)**- When I used to go after a girl I liked, I would go out of my way to find out what kind of guy she liked and fit that mold. It was very rare that I would come forward as just regular old Eric. In my mind, that wasn't good enough. But how do you expect someone to fall in love with an idea of who you are? Its damn near impossible, and if you do happen to win someone over by playing a part, it can only last for so long, because the real you will eventually surface.

1. **Why Does Rejection Hurt-** Rejection sucks, and we all deal with it in different ways. But resenting the person who rejected you just doesn't work. A lot of the anger I felt when women rejected was misunderstood. What I mean by that is, I was inexperienced in understanding my own emotions because I've always been taught that real men were unfeeling. So when a girl I really liked rejected me, I would become really sad and a little depressed. Years of being taught that I wasn't supposed to feel would cause me to punish myself for being emotional. When I couldn't control those emotions, I would begin to resent the person who caused me that pain. I didn't want to acknowledge that I was hurt, so I would go to the easiest and "manliest emotion" anger. But anger solves nothing.

## Can You Afford Me

**Current Playlist:**
Eminem: Love You More
Papa Roach: Scars
Marilyn Manson: Sweet Dreams
Kanye West: Coldest Winter

Can you afford me? I swear there are some women who should really have a shirt with this question. I know it sounds wrong but anyone who has ever gone on, and paid for a date knows exactly what I'm talking about. Being the gentleman SUCKS! You go out with this girl who may or may not be interested in you, may never speak to you again, may never even let you get to first base, and you have to spend all of this money just so on the outside chance she had fun, you can have another opportunity to crucify your wallet by taking her out on a second date.

Ok, so maybe I'm exaggerating a bit, but allow me to paint a picture. Boy meets girl, boy likes girl, girl sees boy and may or may not like him. However, she does think he's

"Kind of cute" or "Kind of cool", so they decide to go on a date. From what I understand, a man is supposed to front the cost of most dates, so we'll assume that for this first date we're doing it simple; dinner and a movie. I don't know about other places, but New York is expensive. You can't take a classy lady out to a fast food joint, chain restaurants may be out of the question too, which means no sticky wings. So now you're forced to be creative and find something that will keep her entertained, well fed, and not put a dent in your wallet. On top of that, you still have to talk to her and laugh at her jokes and get her to laugh at your shitty jokes too. It's too much pressure, I just don't know if I can handle that.

But that rant is not what we're here to discuss. Let's get to the main point. This chapter talks about a girl, but unlike other relationships, she is not the driving factor of the story. But just to get things out of the way, I'll start it off with her.

# Patricia

Patricia like many of my girlfriends was way out of my league. She was 5'9, with straight brown hair, full lips, really white teeth, and very petite (She had amazing tits). Her mother was Puerto Rican, and her Father was Haitian so she had all of the best parts of the island in her features including the sexy high cheek bones and the kind of eyes that told you that she was DTF and exceptionally good at it. Looks aside, Patricia had three things that I absolutely love in women: attitude, ambition, and an interest in me.

Remember when I complained at the beginning of this chapter about how expensive it is to take girls out?

Well Patricia and I hung out the entire night and I spent a total of $20. We met up at 42nd street; window-shopped, ate ice cream, admired the amazing apartments in Soho, and walked across the Brooklyn Bridge. The conversation flowed, and the more we talked the more we liked each other. The date started at 8:00pm, we split up to go our separate ways at 8:00am the next morning. I'm sure I don't need to say it, but yes. I was in love and called her two hours later to make her my girlfriend.

For this period of my life, I was attending a college that I would later learn was a waste of my hard earned money, financial aid, and credit score. We shall call it "FML University". With college comes new friends, new mature friends. I had two of them, Ross and Noah. Ross is one of my favorite people in the world, he's one of those guys that always know way more then he should, he's always down for a good laugh, loyal to a fault, and is the only man I know who can associate relationship experience with Dragon Ball Z Power Levels.

Noah for lack of better words is an asshole. Not to me and Ross of course, but still women love and loath this man all at once. During the first week of school, he peed in the mini fridge of our RA after he wrote us up for playing our music too loud. He's not what you would call the most socially aware or considerate person. He has, on multiple occasions, fallen asleep stark naked in a complete stranger's bed.

After that first date, Patricia and I wasted no time making things official. My days, which had once been spent rampaging through campus with Ross and Noah, were now being used to get quality phone time with Patricia. They could both tell I was wildly infatuated with this girl, and did the only thing a real bro should, they told me to sleep with her. Did I mention that up to this point I was still a virgin? Yeah that's right, yours truly had yet to visit the promise land, and everyone (thanks to Noah) knew of this and was fully invested in fixing the problem.

Noah tried to make sure I used Patricia as my vagina vessel and nothing more.
Patricia and I couldn't wait to see each other so we agreed that she would spend the night on campus the following week. Everything was in place and before you knew it the day

had arrived. Noah and Ross were more excited than a teenage girl at a Justin Bieber concert. I, on the other hand, was as nervous as any sane man could be.

When she arrived, the nerves magically dissipated, she had a way of calming them, and it was only a matter of time before we were arm in arm loving every second of the others company. When Ross, and Noah met her they were floored, I did my very best to describe, her but I don't think they believed me.

*"Ross, Noah, this is my girlfriend Patricia. Babe, this is Ross and Noah"*

*"Oh my god, it's so nice to meet you guys, Eric is always talking about you two"*

At that moment another friend of ours named Brunson walked into the room, Ross and Noah were not fans of him at all.

*"Hey bro aren't you going to introduce your girlfriend to your big brother/ mentor?"*

*"What do you want Dick sweat? (Ross and Noah called him this as a joke, they found it more appealing than Brunson) we don't want to play Halo, so go jerk off with your X Box Controller"*

"Broman, this is Eric's girlfriend Patricia. See she exists. Maybe if you get far enough in Zelda you will win a special ruby that creates a girlfriend for you"

*"Hey I'm Brunson, Eric's big bro"*

*"Hi I'm Tricia, nice to meet you"*

*"Likewise, I'm disappointed my lil bro didn't mention you earlier"*

You know that moment where two people meet, and you can practically see the lust jumping from their skin? Yeah, I had the front row seat of that between Tricia and Brunson. There was an obvious attraction there, one that neither was trying to hide, but at that point I decided to ignore it.

"Tricia this is Brunson, he's one of my best friends and I gotta be honest he's taught me a lot (We'll get to what I said later) so treat him like you would treat family".

Now here is where things start to get interesting. I had class until 8:00 and Tricia wanted to see the campus. Brunson offered to keep her company while I was away so I gladly accepted the offer. I didn't see her again until 3 in the morning when she came to my dorm room to sleep.

*"So um.... What were you and Brunson doing with all that time, I couldn't find you?"*

*-Oh nothing babe, we went to lunch, hung out at the gym, went to this erotic massage program, then sat in his room and talked".*

*(Confused) "Couldn't you guys talk tomorrow, I really wanted to spend some time with you today, I literally have not seen you since 12:00 this afternoon"*

*(glowing) "I know babe, but I have to leave early tomorrow so I decided to hang with Brunson, you and*

*I will have plenty of time to hang out. Brunson spoke so highly of you; he never thought you had it in you to get a girl like me. He told me he regrets not going to that party because if he did I might be with him instead"*

*(in a quiet whisper) "Would you?"*

*" Well maybe, he's more my type then you, but who cares? I saw you and I'm happy with you"*

*(Relieved) "Oh ok cool babe, let's get to bed"*

You guys still with me? Good, don't go far. So Patricia and I go to sleep, and the next day she has breakfast with Brunson and then leaves campus for Brooklyn. I trusted Tricia, I really did, but there was just something about the way she was always talking about Brunson that made me get a funny feeling. But I powered through. Two weeks into the relationship, Tricia told me she loved me, I said it back, because, falling in love with someone you just met is completely reasonable, especially when 85% of your correspondence takes place over the phone.

Despite this newfound love things were getting weird between us. I was constantly busy with college stuff, so we only had time to talk during the night. But when we did speak we would stay on the phone for an hour and then she would tell me she was going to bed.

I was a 19-year-old college student; our phone conversations would be over by 11:30 so I would roam the campus. One night after our phone conversation I went to Brunson's room to hang out, he was on the phone so I hopped on his X Box to play until he finished. Whoever he was talking to it was very obvious that they were having a good time. I tapped him on the shoulder and asked if he wanted me to leave.

"Hey dude, do you want me to get out of here"?

*"Nope its cool, I'm on the phone with Tricia"*

*(Confused) "My Tricia?"*

*" No my Tricia. Yes your Tricia dumb ass, say hi to her so we can finish our conversation"*

I was too confused to do much more then say hello and pass him back the phone. I had a million thoughts in my head as I walked out of his room. "Why were those two on the phone at 3 in the morning, why did she tell me she was going to bed then call him, how did she get his number, or did he get hers, how long had this been going on, and why had no one told me"?

When I asked Patricia about it she brushed it off as two friends talking; when I approached Brunson about it he apologized and said he would never talk to her again if I wanted. I felt bad for causing a scene and told them that I didn't see anything wrong with it.

As time progressed I heard from Patricia less, she claimed she was busy working, but Brunson always knew where she was, what was going on, and what the new inside joke was at her job. I started to see the writing on the wall, but chose to look the other way and enjoy the ride. People will always tell you how great it is to fall in love. No one tells you what happens when you finally hit the floor.

Thursday, it was a Thursday afternoon. No matter how many years it's been I can still remember this day like it was yesterday. I had tests all day and was worn out from a long week of mid terms. Brunson and I hadn't had much time to talk because he was always busy doing one thing or another, while Tricia was trying to handle her crazy course load. I had finished my last exam of the day and was in the school cafeteria scarfing down a sandwich when he broke the news to me.

*"I'm sleeping with Tricia"*

Brunson told me the truth about him and Patricia, about how they talked on the phone every day after she told me she was going to bed, how they both shared a mutual interest in each other, how he wanted to be with her, and she felt the same way. He showed me a conversation they had on msn chat where they were discussing the future of their relationship. At some point during this conversation I guess he felt guilty because he asked:

*"What about Eric"*

Her response was

*"What about him, Eric is great but he's not what I'm looking for in the long term, I'll break up with him for you"*

If you're going to find out that the person you're dating is cheating on you, it's probably not a good idea to read a transcript of the conversation that finalized her decision. Not if you weren't prepared to have your heart ripped out of your ass. I didn't react, instead I sat there and got an earful on how I was not wanted.

*"Sorry man, she doesn't want to be with you. We talked about it and I'm more of her type. I know you're probably upset but you gotta know that if I was at that party you would of never had a chance with her. She and I have a date this Saturday, and we want to make it official and become a couple, but I need you to break up with her and give me your blessing. You're my little brother and I love you to*

*death, but you can't hand a girl like her, this is the*
*way its supposed to be! I hope you're not mad at me"*

*"She doesn't want to be with me?"*

*"She doesn't, said she went out with you because she*
*didn't want to hurt your feelings by saying no when*
*you asked her out, I can make her happy and you*
*can't. That's not your fault, its just the way it is".*

The rest of that dinner was a blur, but just to
sum it up, I spent the rest of the time making
believe that I was ok with how things went
down. I gave Brunson my blessing to date her,
and tried to laugh at the entire ordeal like it
was a big joke to me, it was not.

Later that night I called Patricia and told her
about everything that Brunson told me, she
confirmed most of it, trying to clean up her
part in the ordeal so she wouldn't seem like
such a mean person.

*"So you never liked me, what was it, am I not good*
*looking enough for you?"*

*"That's not it at all, you're a great guy, and I really enjoyed our time together, but I can't lie to you and say that Brunson and I don't have something that I want to pursue"*

*"I thought you loved me"*

*"I do love you, I really do but Brunson and I talked about this and he's right, its better that I hurt your feelings now before I break your heart later. You're not supposed to be with a girl like me. You need a nice girl, because you're a nice guy"*

*"If I'm such a nice guy, why don't you want to be with me, I know I don't have a lot of money or the best clothes but we talked about that, I said I would get better"*

*"It's not about that, you're fine the way you are, just not meant for me"*

She and I broke up that night at 1:37am; she and Brunson officially became a couple at 2:00am, less than 30 minutes after she had confirmed I wasn't good enough for her, she already had her replacement and I had a reason to have a broken heart. There was a party on campus that night, Ross and Noah were somewhere with the rest of our friends having the time of their lives. I stayed in my dorm room. I could hear people in the hallways, they sounded like the world was perfect; I hated them because my world had just imploded. I wanted so badly to cry that night. I stayed in bed all night with the door locked, all of the lights off, along with the TV and radio, and replayed that entire relationship in my head. I started to realize that she always seemed to insert Brunson into our conversations. He always knew what was going on between us. He had a laptop and I couldn't afford one, so they were constantly on video chat together. The signs were all there and I ignored them. I should have seen this coming from a mile away, but I didn't. Tricia and Brunson's words kept replaying in my head, and as every minute passed by I hated myself more for being so weak.

## Wait, There's More

Wouldn't it be great if this were the end of the story? Well guess what, we're not done yet. The next morning Brunson left campus to meet up with Tricia in the city. When I woke up that morning it took me a moment to remember and then process what had happened just a few hours earlier. The minute it sunk in I was rocked with depression. I sat up in my bed and tried to collect my thoughts and emotions. After all, I had promised Brunson and Tricia that I wouldn't tell anyone what happened between the three of us.

I spent the next couple of weeks suffering through one of the most pitiful times of my life. The semester was coming to an end, there was a party on campus every night and although, I had at one time been very social, I became a recluse. Every day was spent in class or in my dorm room. I tried to act like nothing was wrong with me, but everyone knew something was up, I walked around campus with a CD player and the only album I listened to was "Scars" from Papa Roach.

Those lyrics defined every emotion that I tried to hide from my closest friends. But like any good bro, Ross and Noah knew exactly what happened. Things came to a head on a Thursday night. Ross and Noah were drunk out of there minds, and were trying to walk to the girls dormitory, In a half hearted attempt to stop them I grabbed Ross and told him to "Cool it" but because he was chocolate wasted he decided it would be a good time to confront me about my angst.

*Come on man, you've been walking around here like someone threw sand in your vagina for weeks! Get over it, walk it off!*

Ross may have been drunk but he was absolutely right. Just when things were about to settle down Patricia's voice broke through the chaos.

*"What the hell is going on here, Eric are you fighting?!"*

There were about 20 people in my dorm suite; all of them were focused on Tricia. Noah in a drunken stupor broke the awkward silence by making the situation slightly worse.

*- "Yo ain't you Eric's Bitch?!*

A few people in the room chuckled silently but seemed to recognize her as my girlfriend. Most people didn't know what happened yet; well they didn't until Brunson walked into the suite.

*Actually Noah, She's not Eric or anyone's Bitch, her name is Tricia and since she's my girlfriend you should probably watch how you talk to her.* Eric, Tricia is spending the night, can she borrow a pair of your shorts to sleep in?"

The room stared at him in shock and disgust, but I'm sure my reply was the saddest expression of manhood in collegiate history.

*"Um yeah, I just did laundry so I have some, do you guys need condoms too?"*

*"My man, that's exactly what I need!"*

At this point everyone in the room including Tricia was looking at me like I had three heads. Brunson may have taken advantage of my pathetic state, but I was the one who gave him every opening to do so.

Here is something that you should understand. I gave Tricia and Brunson my blessing and they took it and ran, so while I may have had every reason to be pissed at what was taking place, I felt like I should just let it roll off my back. If I reacted by getting upset, yelling, cursing, or attempting violence I would just look weak and petty. I chose perception over reality, and to convince everyone that I was ok I stabbed myself with a metaphorical knife, then dug it in and twisted it with a smile on my face hoping that people would see the smile and assume that all was right. Unfortunately for me, college students may be drunks but they're not stupid. The only person being fooled by this act was me.

After the condom offer, Tricia looked at me with the saddest eyes I had ever seen, her glare was so piercing I had to put my head down to avoid her. I don't know if it was regret, remorse or a combination of both, but she was not happy. I don't know when it happened but eventually I gave up on trying to look like everything was ok, I completely fell apart and that's when I started to move on.

## Hindsight is 20/20

I learned a lot of things about myself. Tricia and Brunson broke up a few days after that incident; he told her he wasn't ready to fall in love. They had an on again off again relationship for the next two years, Brunson and I remained friends but things were never the same. Tricia was persistent and fought hard to stay in my life, and for a long time I hated her for what she did, and I don't think she'll ever be able to give me a real answer as to why she chose Brunson over me, but we moved beyond that and have become really good friends. But the mistakes from that relationship will always be with me. If you don't see yourself as an asset, how do you expect anyone else to? Brunson and Patricia could do what they did because I valued them more than I did myself. Sure they were dicks for how things went down, but having a little backbone goes a long way.

# The Virginity Story

**Current Playlist:**

Papa Roach: Infest

Same Cooke: Change

Papa Roach: No more Secrets

I've been struggling to find the right words to talk about this. Does that even make sense? Well its true. Who wants to be the guy that has everyone's attention and then screws it up by telling a really shitty story? That can't be me, well it could, but I'm trying to avoid that. You're supposed to find out how I finally lost my V Card, that means virginity people. I would also like to use this as an opportunity to admit to just how sad, lonely and low I was when it happened. Did I say sad, lonely, and low? I didn't mean it that way, I guess the best way to put it is that I didn't have an identity; not yet anyway. It was like being in a shoe store trying to find the right pair of sneakers. But you don't know what size you wear, and you have no idea where to find the sneakers. You end up roaming around just going for whatever looks or feels good. That's how I was, I latched onto whatever looked and felt good, I did the same thing with friends, school, life, goals and of course women. So it's a bit surprising that it took me until I was 20 years old to actually lose my virginity. But It did, lets get into that.

I think I could make a fifty-page list on why it took me so long to lose my virginity. One of the biggest factors was that I was extremely shy. Not shy in conventional standards, when it came to engaging in conversations I could do that, and I wasn't afraid to approach strange women, that was also a piece of cake, but when it came time to seal the deal for the romantic stuff, I was lost, mostly because I didn't know how to not look like a creep. This shyness stopped me from approaching plenty of women I may have actually had a chance to get with; it stunted my experience as well. So while many of my friends had already had been to third base (Under the shirt, no bra) I was still working up the guts to go for a French kiss. I didn't know how to talk to women, I didn't really know how to be around them, and doing anything besides being snarky and a little awkward was asking a lot from me. How do you know what to do when you're with a girl? Girls are confusing and complicated. I would stress over how to go from a friendly conversation to sex without looking like a creeper, and the formula wasn't clear at all. By the time I got to college this was still a problem, one that I needed to address, so I started practicing tactics on my female friends. If it worked on them I assumed it would work on others. But I was still mostly shy. It was weird, because around my friends I was this outgoing creature that spoke as if he had a 15-inch penis along with an iron clad trust fund. Everyone was under the perception that I was this big womanizer, and I wasn't. The decision to lose my virginity was one that came from more shame than want.

Any and everyone who knew that I was still a virgin (and that was everyone) would make fun of me, I'm sure they hadn't meant to be mean, but there are only so many times that you can be called a "Fucking Virgin" before the insult starts to sting a little bit. During my intro to psychology class someone decided to tell the professor that I hadn't had sex yet. She (the professor) thought this was amazing and gave us an assignment in which each individual group had to come up with a theory as to why I wasn't getting laid. For the next two hours, I listened to group theories on why I hadn't had sex yet. There was even a top ten lists made. I think this was the turning point. I could be wrong, but I distinctly remember making a decision when the professor pulled me aside after class and offered to let me "give her a go" so I could get some mileage under my belt.

Reasons That Eric is Still a Virgin

1. Super small dick
2. Prefers sex with trees and shrubbery
3. Is Gay
4. Is Gay
5. Is Gay and also Gay
6. Smells like balls
7. Is afraid of The clam sandwich

## Sex is… Interesting

I remember every single detail from the day I lost my virginity. It was a balmy 50 degrees, and the day after Thanksgiving, Monique who I hadn't seen since my senior year of High School invited me over to her place. She and I hadn't really talked much since that awesome time she made out with her girlfriend while I was her boyfriend.) But she had my number and begged me to come over. According to her, she "missed what we had". I'm not sure what exactly it was that she missed, but I had nothing and wanted absolutely nothing from her; except for maybe a hand job. Yes, I was still at the age where hand jobs were something I hoped to receive from women. Getting a hand job is still leaps and bounds more interesting than masturbating. Almost like the way playing tennis is better than handball. When you're playing Tennis it's always a little more intense, because you have someone else there and anything can happen. In Handball you slap your ball against the wall until your hand gets sore (See what I did there). Nothing much else besides the usual will happen. Get my point? So I agreed to go see her. She lived in some obscure part of Brooklyn, until then I thought I had been to every corner and crevice of my favorite borough, but clearly this was a location bordering next to ratchet Narnia. I found her apartment building and quickly made my way up. Before I could knock on her door she had tossed it open and pulled me into a big hug, I let her go and stepped into her apartment. It wasn't that big, and it definitely wasn't that interesting (but that's not what we're here for now is it). However, there were two things that stood out to me; ok, maybe three. The first was that her mother was sitting right in the living room, and was in crutches. She had fallen down some stairs a week earlier and was now camped out in the living room because her room didn't have cable. The second was that she had a little brother who couldn't have been any older than 2. He kept busy by running up and down the apartment pulling doors open; the third and final thing was something I figured out when we got to her room. Monique didn't have a lock on her door. She could close it, but at any moment any person could just walk up to her door and open it without ever thinking about knocking first, and her little brother didn't seem like a door knocking type. I quickly gave up my dreams of getting a hand job. It was obvious that it couldn't happen under such circumstances. I blocked out all thoughts of Monique's hands making contact with my lower regions from my mind; it wasn't going to happen. But there is something really funny about life. When you make a plan for something that you really want, that plan will more than likely go straight to hell. But when you leave things be and just take what's given to you, shit can get pretty interesting. Well in this case, things got really interesting really quick. Monique had an ulterior motive for bringing me here, and she wasted no time in putting her plan to action.

*"I can't believe you're here, I have missed you so much, when was the last time we actually just hung out Eric?"*

*I know what you mean; I haven't heard a thing from you that time you made out with your girlfriend even though you were supposed to be dating me.*

*Yeah, I'm still sorry about that. I didn't know I was gay back then, well at least I didn't know I was that gay…. But that's why I invited you over; I want to make that up to you… right now.*

She straddled me and we started making out. That sounds really hot right? Well it wasn't; I for one had no idea what I was doing, and if memory recalls correctly I lathered her face with lots of saliva, and spit on her face at least three times. Things were moving pretty quick, and before I knew it we were both in our underwear; ok she was in her underwear, and I had my pants at my ankles but my jacket was still on. I remember being so worried that I was going to do something wrong, that I didn't have time to process exactly what was happening. Every move was thought out, I tried tricks that I saw in porno movies. If figured if **Dirty Nancy** liked to be called a "cock gobbler" that's probably what I should call Monique.

*You ready for this Cock Gobbler?*
 *What the hell did you just call me?*
*Uh, I called you a cock gobbler.*
 My plan wasn't working that well,  I was
hoping that Monique would take the lead but
she wasn't, and my attempt to turn her on
with porno themed dirty talk had failed
miserably.
*Why would you call me a "Cock gobbler" I've never
gobbled a cock before; now if you're talking about a
snatch attacker, that's me 100%.*

 I'm sure comments like that coming from the
woman you were about to sleep with would
sound pretty awesome to most guys, but for
me it just killed whatever chance of romance
there could have been in this scenario.  After
some more awkward fooling around, it was
time to get down to business. But I couldn't
get into the experience, something was off, in
every scene of porn I had ever watched, there
was music playing, we needed a soundtrack to
have sex, that's how you know in the porno's
that the crappy dialogue is over and it's Go
time. Luckily, Monique had a stereo set in her

room and it already had a CD loaded. Unfortunately, it was a kid CD with only one song on it. I was going to have sex for the first time ever with "If You're Happy and You Know it" playing as my soundtrack. It took me less than 30 seconds to realize that I didn't have any condoms but Monique was prepared. She had a box of ribbed magnums under her pillow. I guess she wanted to be sexy, because she tried to put the condom on me, but instead of using her hands she tried to go for the mouth trick. It failed and she ended up going into a 67 second coughing fit. Eventually I got the condom on, but that wasn't the end of our troubles. In most pornos, the guy is grossly out of shape and super ugly, but the girl is smoking hot and has an awesome body. Monique had let herself go since High School, things didn't look as good today as they did two chapters ago. I spent another five minutes trying to find the hole (SERIOUSLY), and then there's penetration. On porn hub, penetration is always super theatrical, and the girl amplifies that by making all sorts of erotic noises and telling you how big your cock is. I know it sounds ridiculous now, but I was kind of expecting something along those lines to happen, can you blame me? Porn has been the only way I've ever been able to learn about sex, before porn streaming I thought blue balls was an STD.

You know how in all of those teen movies, when the couple lose their virginity its really tender, and soft, and super loving? More often than not there is a really cheesy Creed song being played in the background, and the entire scene is a 5-minute montage of the missionary position and steady eye contact. My first time wasn't like that at all. In reality, I had one foot inside of Monique (Metaphorically) and the other foot was positioned to sprint, just incase her mother decided to magically have her foot healed and barge into the room. She was making a lot of noise and couldn't seem to control her movements, and I spent 15 minutes of my life trying to figure out at which point during this process I stopped being a virgin. I should be clear about something, sex is great, but the way everyone

I knew talked about it, I thought it was going to be this life changing experience that would make me look at everything differently. I thought it would feel like my dick was struck by lightning, but in a way that felt really good and wouldn't leave any long-term trauma, and yes while sex is good and even great. It's not as world breaking as so many people had me believe when I was a virgin.

I probably should have suspected that this sexual experience wasn't going to be grand when Monique looked at my penis and laughed.

But I didn't. Instead I exhaled internally and decided to keep going. My next hint should have been when she asked me if we could "scissor". Would you judge me if I said I actually tried it? Ok never mind. If those two instances weren't enough to tell you that this sexual tryst was going in the wrong direction, how about that she kept yelling out the names of random women the entire time? I want to say I was offended, but I really didn't care, I knew I didn't want anything to do with her and it was kind of nice to know that I wouldn't owe her a phone call after. She had a blast, making weird noises and screaming out for "Sally" and "Becca". I don't know if Monique had fun. I was only moderately entertained, but mostly disappointed, she made none of the porno sounds, the music CD was starting to skip, and she didn't know any of the tricks that my favorite XXX actors did. I didn't know any tricks either, but I'm the guy, I shouldn't have to work.

**Romantic much?** Just as I finished, her little brother barged into the room. I was already dressed so there was nothing to see, but after that close call we decided I should probably go home. I remember sitting on the bus thinking about a meal I had at a local diner just a week ago. For whatever reason I had this weird craving for hot wings, but not just any kind of hot wings. I wanted something classy; I wanted the sticky wings from Dallas BBQ's. I knew that the diner wouldn't have sticky wings, but at the time I was so desperate for wings, I decided to take a chance on them. Long story short, the wings sucked, they sucked monumentally and I was so ticked off that I complained to the waiter. They apologized for the shitty wings, gave me a full refund and brought out a fresh batch of wings that would be comped off of my bill. I couldn't help sitting on the bus during that ride home, wishing I could go back to Monique's apartment and ask for my virginity back. With no disrespect meant towards her, I wasted something of that magnitude on someone whom I barely had a care for. I gave up my virginity to a girl I hadn't spoken to in almost three years, and the only reason I did it was so I could get people at my college to stop making fun of me. I wasn't happy on that bus ride home; I was actually ashamed, embarrassed, and empty. But hey, at least I wasn't a virgin anymore… right?

# Performance Anxiety

**Current Playlist:**

My Chemical Romance: Mama
Maxwell: Fist Full of Tears
Destiny's Child: Bugaboo
Lonely Island Boys: Jizz in my pants.
Jay Z: Big Pimpin

Ok this is going to get very uncomfortable very fast, but it's something that I really need to address. Has any guy ever suffered from performance anxiety? Wait no, don't laugh, I don't mean like not being able to "get it up", or "blowing your load" before you even break skin. I'm talking about just being really nervous about having sex with a girl. You want to have sex with her, and she wants you in and around her vagina but in the back of your mind there are fears that you won't be able to satisfy her, or even worse you won't be big enough for her; oh so that's just my personal issue?

I'm sure you're all laughing at me, but one of my greatest fears is that I'm about to have sex with the girl of my dreams, and just as I drop my pants, she gets a good look at what I'm working with, and then laughs uncontrollably. Am I the only one who heard girls talking about what they expected from guys in bed, and was just a little intimidated? I once heard a girl tell a group of her friends that if a guy wasn't at least twelve inches long, and had enough willpower to not cum for at least two hours, she would not only stop sleeping with him, but would inform the community that he was a limp dick failure. I don't know about the rest of you, but I'm not twelve inches, the last I checked only horses, whales and mutants get that big. But she had a very active sex life so was she bluffing or am I just the only guy who didn't have a penis at least twelve inches long?!

I never really had the "Birds and Bees" talk with my dad. Any sex talk he ever had with me was grossly traumatizing or confusing. I remember when on my 16th birthday he talked about using condoms.

Dad: *Remember that girl from down the hall?*
Me: *Amanda?*

*Dad: Yeah the 22 year old. I've been banging her since Christmas, it was great, she's small so I bounce her all over the house and slam her into things. It was the best piece of ass I had in a while. Until I went to the doctor and found out I had the clap. That's when I realized that you have to use condoms in America, it's not like back home.*

No one with an IQ level above 90 would consider this a legitimate birds and bees talk. My only option for information was friends from school, and it consisted mostly of one of the guys bragging about how good he gave it to some chick. If I had to talk, I would just tell the same generic lie, because seriously what 16-year-old boy is going to admit that

A.     He didn't know what to do, and B. He was a virgin?

Besides being the worst possible option for sex advice, my dad was a bit judgmental, when he was my age he was having sex like stopping would end the world. What would he think if he found out his son was well into his first year of college before reaching third base?

I couldn't mention that to him, he would have probably thought I was gay. I remember I introduced him to Clara and after she left he asked me how far we got. I told him we only kissed; he stopped speaking to me for a week.

I've been sexually active and have never received a complaint, but girls are so partisan when you're her boyfriend. She's blinded by emotion and obligation so if she say's you're the best she's ever had and that you're the size of a small whale you should probably take those comments with a grain of salt; I do. And then I found a solution. Until I was fully confident in my vagina pounding skills I could just sleep with a bunch of women to build up my stamina! All I had to do was find a venue where women in their early twenties would A. Not know me at all, and B. Totally down for the cause of letting me sleep with them for practice. In 2005, there was only one place you could go to find a great deal like that.

## Internet Dating

Full disclosure; I have never really tried Internet dating and if I'm anywhere near as awesome as I feel, I will never have to. But on the list of ways to meet people, this is the simplest, least intimidating and efficient way to do so. Now you must also remember this was early 2005 the internet was popular, but social networks were just beginning to blow up, so the people on these sites were still 70% actual people and not just internet robots programmed to get you to send 200 dollars to them for their sick mother in Africa. I found a site that promised to supply me with plenty of beautiful women with daddy issues then began my web search.

# Jennifer

The first thing I noticed about Jennifer was her ass, and then her breasts. She had one of those nice plump asses that have been whipped into shape from hours of squats and lunges, and her breast were young firm and perky. It was clear they had yet to be damaged by the toils of life, domestic beer, and father time. Now her face.... Well her face was a completely different story. She wasn't hideous, but to call her beautiful would be a lie. She was also the first Cuban woman I ever dated and is the reason I will never again believe that all Cuban women are exotic, beautiful, and **sweat cocaine?**... Wait forget it, that's my stereotype for Colombian women, and it has yet to be proven wrong! But anyway she was a fair skinned with dirty blond hair (Very dirty) cold boring brown eyes, thin lips, and really messed up teeth. No seriously the inside of her mouth looked like a cave. It looked like she tried to give a blowjob to a hammer and bit down; her teeth looked like oatmeal before you cook it. But, she had a very sexy voice, with a killer body so you can be sure I looked right past the cracked egg shells she called the inside of her mouth. Jennifer and I chatted it up for days with AOL instant messenger, and then talked all night on the phone. Don't let the constant conversation fool you I hated her. She had no personality and outside of lusty talk she wasn't what you would call the girl of my dreams. But when it was time for Lusty talk, Man oh man this girl was by far the dirtiest, nastiest, freakiest girl I had ever spoken to. She was the Michael Jordan of phone boning (Yes, that's a thing, or it was before snap chat). We decided that talking would not be enough and planned for her to visit me on campus that Friday which gave me four days to strategize. I went to the man who has a proven record of random hook ups, Noah.

*I got a random coming over Friday, how does this work?*


*Wait, you told her where you live?*

*Yeah*

*Man what the hell is wrong with you, what if she has like Lupus or something?!*

*What?! Noah you know Lupus isn't contagious right?*

*Ok but she could have Aids though, you need to be safe, take her to a Hotel*

*Not to be a dick but, I don't think taking her to a different location would stop me from contracting Aids or HIV. Could you just give me some advice and stop being weird?*

*Ok this is easy, have condoms on deck, a fresh pair of bed sheets you can throw away later, clean your room, have money to order pizza and pay for a cab, shave your pubes and jerk off before she gets there.*

*You had me until you mentioned those last two things on the check list.*

*Listen Floppy Cock, I know what I'm talking about. Do you like it when a girl is all Bush? Exactly, so keep yours shaved too. Girls like that; it shows you considered them, and chicks appreciate classy stuff like that.*

*Ok fine but what about the jerking off thing, isn't that kind of counterproductive?*

*When was the last time you had sex? If it was over a week ago then you need to jerk off. If not you're going to be finished two minutes after you started I promise.*

I nodded in agreement but secretly I was really beginning to question his twisted logic. The big day was finally here and Jennifer was in my dorm room. Small talk was out of the question, she came over in a micro mini skirt with no panties, and tank top ;dick was on her menu and I was serving it. Despite his vigilant effort to warn me, I only listened to half of the two biggest warnings, Jennifer was very happy about the special haircut.

*Oh my god you shaved!*

*Yeah uh... You don't like it, I did this for you.*

*Um hell yeah I love it! You don't know how annoying it is to get pubes stuck in your teeth.*

I would like to take a moment to allow you to gag, and possibly judge me if you have not done so already... Finished? Ok good. She, just as Noah said, thanked me with a courtesy blow job, the time for sex was quickly arriving and I was ready, I didn't squeeze one out like Noah suggested, but who cares? I felt weird doing that after some guy instructed me to. What if I listened and when I went to do it he was somewhere nodding his head in approval? The funny thing about Noah is that even though he's a jerk 9/10 times if he warns you about something, it's because he knows what he's talking about. 45 seconds into the act Jen started to moan out some kind of incoherent dirty talk. To be honest the only thing I made out completely were; *"Ya, Oatmeal Deep"*. 46 and a half seconds later I was a goner. I remember feeling the inevitable coming and trying to fight it off. My last words were "NOOOOOO". I tried to keep going like nothing happened, but this is a girl who's seen more dicks than Hanes underwear, she knows what that sound is for. She didn't even bother speaking. Just put on her clothes and left in disgust. I had no one to blame but myself. I tried contacting her a few days later and her response wasn't very polite or encouraging.

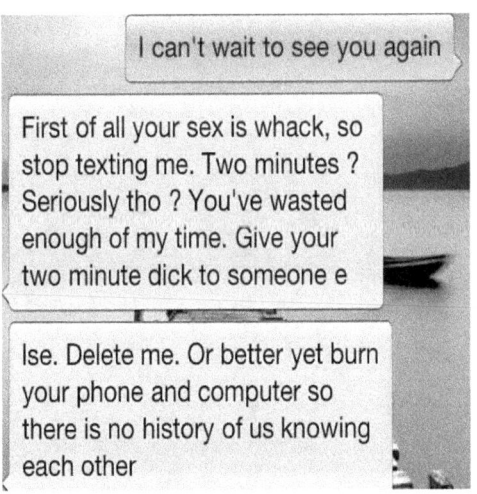

I can't wait to see you again

First of all your sex is whack, so stop texting me. Two minutes ? Seriously tho ? You've wasted enough of my time. Give your two minute dick to someone e

lse. Delete me. Or better yet burn your phone and computer so there is no history of us knowing each other

Later on that night I told Noah the story, he laughed his self into a mini asthma attack then made me buy him a bag of weed to apologize for almost killing him.

*Ok limp dick, take this (Passes box). It's called "Super Strokes". You pop two of these and I promise you there will be no killing your boner. But read the fine print before you use it.*

## Why I will never not read the fine print again.

After her very hurtful message, I actually convinced Jen to come over again for some redemption dick. About 30 minutes before she arrived I started prepping myself for the rematch. With five minutes to spare before she walked in I popped two "Long Strokes". Jen came in five minutes later. As usual she was not one for words, she walked into my room straddled me and we started making out but something was wrong and not like semi wrong but very wrong. Jen and I were getting pretty hot and steamy but my soldier wouldn't stand at full attention. When she finally noticed she gave me a confused look, so I used a line Brett swears he tells every girl. "Its time for you tuh suck dis dick!"

Jen must love directions because she followed orders like the fate of the world depended on it. Her sucking skills were high quality but I still couldn't get it up. About ten minutes into her blowing me I grabbed the "Super Strokes" bottle and read the fine print.

"Warning, Super Strokes should be used at the peak of an erection, do not use before erection repeat do not use before erection"

To sum it up for you guys, the way this pill worked was that it latched on to an already raging boner and just maintained it. All it does is heighten whatever state you're in and maintain it. So if you're soft and you take this pill well I think you can guess what this means for me.

Jen figured this out very fast, stared at my lifeless package gave me a look of pure contempt and walked out of the room.
I thought about letting it go but this was bad. There was no way I could let a girl leave my room with that perception of me. In order to save face, I needed to respond as quickly as possible and be forthright about what happened. So like any guy embarrassed about his performance, I waited about a week before I tried contacting her again.

## Dick Steroids and the Bugaboo

*Hey uh... Can we talk about the other day?*

*Ok, so it wasn't my fault. I took these pill and they made me get weird, I was trying to make sure I did well for you and the pills were supposed to be like dick steroids, but they failed, not me.*

*That's your big explanation?!*

*That's really what happened... Can you give me another chance?*

I'll never forget her response.

*" You Buggin what, you buggin who, you buggin me and don't you see it ain't cool Even if the pope says he likes you too I don't really care cause you're a Bug a boo"*

That my friends, is how I got dumped with the lyrics from Destinies Childs Bugaboo

## Sex, Women and Lessons
**Current Playlist:**
The Dream: Mr. Yeah
Gym Class Heros: Cookie Jar
Trey Songz: Scratching Me Up


Virgins suck Ok, maybe that was a bit too aggressive, but if forced to make a list of the type of women I would l like to have sex with, virgins don't even make the list. On the top of that list would be a girl who has a healthy sexual resume. Which really means I'm looking for a sexual deviant. Trust me, sex with a woman who knows what she's doing and enjoys sex as much as you do will always be the best sex you can have. Whoever told you that having sex with virgins is the cool thing to do is a creepy poser who likes to bang inexperienced women so he can feel better about his self. Why would you want to go through that? Why would anyone want to engage in any kind of fortification with someone who has no idea what they're doing? Sex doesn't come with instruction manuals, oh and by the way, most women are in pain while losing their virginity. I hear in some countries, people will go to war because some guy promised them virgins in the afterlife! They can't possibly know what they're getting themselves into.

Is that racist, I hope not? But seriously men need a serious re-education on women. I'll start it off by debunking some of the lies that our stupid guy friends and other sex hating folk have told us over the years.

1. **Women don't like Sex**- Society has built this standard that claims women are not fans of sex. Men are the sex fiends and women just tolerate it. Women enjoy sex, if they didn't why the hell would they ever consent to it?

2. **Casual Sex Can't Work because women always catch feelings-** This is complete bull, but I'll get into that later.

3. **Women with several sexual partners should be considered "sluts" "whores" and generally loose.** .- This is also wrong,

and whoever started this lie should be punched in the nuts.

4. **Sex should only be pleasurable for the man**- Well it can be, but if you're having sex with a bunch of women, and you're the only one walking away from those experiences as a happy camper, it's only a matter of time before no one is going to want to have sex with you anymore.

5. **Sex is just like a porno.**-Sex is nothing like a porno, there are no strobe lights, unless you put the radio on before hand. Techno music does not just magically start, and women don't really shout out "fuck yeah" repeatedly in real life.

Remember these five as my story begins and concludes. It started off at a summer cabin. No, not a summer camp this isn't some sappy teen Disney love movie. Noah had an uncle who owned a cabin in the country. It was next to a beautiful lake, in a town that was used to college students coming into buy alcohol, party, have sex, and go home at summers end.

Me and six other friends decided to spend our summer there. It was Ross, Noah, Brett, three girls, and me: Clair, Becca and Shevon.

The Cabin was huge so we all had our own bedrooms, three bathrooms, two Jacuzzi's, a beautiful patio with a deck built for summer BBQ's, another deck on the second floor with an amazing view of the lake, and a wine cellar filled with all of the old classy shit we could douse our livers in. During the first week all we did was party excessively every single day, invite other college students over and act out the scenes from the project X movie. Eventually things slowed down and we went from partying every night to just three to four times a week. It was during this time that I started to get to know Clair. She was a pretty awesome girl, beautiful, intelligent, and a bit odd. Then again, I generally found any woman willing to sleep with me a bit odd. She was what you would call exotic. Her mother was Taiwanese and her father Nigerian and together they created Clair, a smoking hot mixture of her parents. Taking on her mother's eyes, high cheekbones, and long hair, but she inherited her father's athletic body (That actually sounds kind of creepy) and grandmothers long legs. I don't know what side of the family gave her those lips but they were plum, full and looked really good over..... Ok forget that last part.

Clair would come to my room and we would shoot the shit. It was one of those platonic relationships that made no sense because the people involved got on so well. One day she came into my room and I was depressed about something, I don't even remember what it was anymore, but she came in and decided to lie down with me and cuddle to cheer me up; bad idea.

She and I may have developed a great friendship, but I was still very attracted to her. It was only a matter of minutes before there was an uncomfortable erection between us. And when dealing with a surprise boner there are only three things you can do:

1.  Lay on your stomach and think about baseball until it goes away

2. Position yourself so that she accidentally touches it, then say something real smooth and get your sex on.
3. Freeze from panic then get caught.

*Umm Eric... You feeling a little frisky today?*

*Sorry, just ignore it. It will go away eventually.*

*Oh, so it's not standing at attention because of me?*

*Well I don't want to be the creepy erection guy...*

*It's a little too late for that buddy.*

*Ok sorry I'll go take a walk, I didn't mean to make things weird like that. It's a guy thing sometimes I can't control it.*

*Well it's already hard, so can I at least see it? I haven't gotten any in a while, it will be nice to see one of those things again.*

*You want to see it? Ok whatever.*

You're probably wondering why I was so cool with showing her my junk. Well if you knew what she looked like you would understand. I pulled it out and let her see, she gasped grabbed it with both hands and said;

*"That is the biggest penis I have ever seen!"* (She didn't really say that, but this is my story, deal with it)

I'm not the smartest guy in the world, and this book can document all of my poor decisions, but one of the smartest things I ever did was make a move on Clair. She had already seen my penis and was currently holding it in her hand. I figured I had nothing to lose so I went in for a kiss. She accepted and from there it was on. Don't listen to any movie you have ever watched, sex isn't always this seamless experience, especially when you're having sex with someone for the first time.

In a normal relationship, it's healthy to discuss what you like and dislike, as well as any weird sex habits before you actually engage. This usually helps to smooth out the process.

Claire and I didn't have that opportunity. My kiss took us from zero to 60 and it was on! My kisses were sloppy and a bit desperate, she returned the favor, a bit confused but into it. Claire was not a shy girl. While I was still into the kiss she had already shifted gears and was taking off her clothes. Before I knew it we were in a tangle of sheets and nothing else mattered. That first time only lasted for about 30 minutes (5 minutes), but let me tell you; it was great! The competition in kisses was just the start of our back and forth, we battled for who would be in top, we battled for who would lead the tempo, and then we got into the act and worked double time to out screw the other. It was a satisfying 30 minutes. We both knew that things had changed from then. We lied in silence for a couple of minutes before she broke the ice.

*How did you end up with your face in my vagina?*

*I'm not sure but I think it's a good fit.*

*I think so too, so what is this going to be? I don't want a boyfriend. I'm not interested in being serious right now.*

*Well neither am I, but I really like having sex with you. We should do this again.*

*Oh, so you want to screw me but not make me your girlfriend? Typical guy shit!*

*No, not at all. We can have sex, watch Netflix, and talk, and do everything we've been doing. Just now, we're having sex when there is nothing good on Netflix.*

*Will you still buy me weed and let me sleep over sometimes?*

*Sure.*

*Ok cool, it's a deal.*

And our sexual adventure started just like that. Claire and I had sex everywhere. We did it in the lake, both Jacuzzis, everyone's room, all three bathrooms, the patios backyard, kitchen, weight room and of course on the bed. Nothing was unconventional. Each time we did it was better than the last, and we would go at it for hours then hang out in my room, watching movies and playing video games. We had the ideal set up, and I strongly suggest it to anyone with time and stamina available to do it.  Here is what I liked most about Clara:

1.Claire had an outrageous sex drive. We would go at it for two hours until she couldn't take anymore and 30 minutes after a nap, she would be ready for a rematch.

2.Claire loved giving and receiving Oral sex, and she was good at it and I mean very good. She gave a full throttled effort every time she went down on me and I didn't have to ask or had done something good. She would just be "In the moment"

3. She was very familiar with her body. Claire knew exactly what she liked and how it made her feel so after the first time there was never a moment of miscommunication since we both knew what was coming next.

4. She helped me get past a lot of my sexual hang ups, and become a lot more comfortable with my body and pleasures. After spending years taking advice on women and sex from my stupid guy friends, I finally had an attractive female telling giving me the real details

The summer eventually came to a halt. We probably helped Trojans stock triple with our constant purchase of condoms. When everyone left we stayed an extra day and had one last crazy love fest for the road.

## Hindsight is 20/20

What hindsight? That was an awesome summer. I spent all of my days with a close friend who I cared about like crazy and got to have all kinds of lewd and devious sex. Why would I regret that?

# News Flash

**Current Playlist:**
Eminem: Superman
Equinox: First of The Year
D 12: Pimp Like Me
Scarface Soundtrack: Push it to the limit
Luther Vandross: Superstar


Ok, I've got some breaking news for you, well you might actually know this already, but I'll at least confirm your greatest fears.
Women love assholes and bad boys. Take a second and think about this, because I'm about 98% sure that the women reading this are either shaking their heads in disgust, or laughing because they know it's true.

Think back to any relationship you have ever had, think back to any girl you've ever expressed interest in. Now think of the ones that didn't work out. How many times have you gotten that girl from being cool, easy to talk to, understanding, supportive, and available? You can lie to yourself but please don't lie to me. I'm the epitome of a nice guy, so I know for a fact how far that kind of behavior takes you. Women just like "Bad Boys". They love having an element of danger with their men. A guy who won't express his feelings, won't answer her calls, will ignore her in front of other people, and generally treat her like shit. I'm not making this up, it just is what it is.

I'll use myself as an example. When clean-shaven, I have the look of a stereotypical black guy, possibly dangerous, possibly not. When I have facial hair I tend to have a tougher edge to me. I become a stereotypical black guy with possible armed robbery, and drug charges. Guess which version of me gets the most action. It's so serious that when I have a beard my roommates say that my evil twin brother is living with them. This same beard has assisted me in rounding third base on several occasions. Here's another example. Anyone who really knows me is aware of the fact that I rarely ever get angry or upset; I'm usually in pretty high spirits, but any time I have gotten to the point where I am angry, or bubbling on aggression, most of the females within radius begin to find me deathly attractive. Chicks dig danger.

The nice guy boost her ego, makes her feel good, and supplies emotional support, but the bad boy always gets her, at least in the younger years. But have no fear; there is hope for the good guy. I'm beginning to notice that a lot of women eventually gravitate towards the nicer men after multiple traumatic relationships, or their biological clock starts ticking. With the first, this can be a toss up for the good guy, because although she's ready to date you, there is a strong likelihood that she's settling because you're a safe pick, and even more of a chance that you'll have to deal with all of the emotional, and trust issues that the "Bad Boys" helped her to accrue. Every man/woman wants to get the girl, but very few of us want to be told they're with us because we're "safe"; I wouldn't call that a ringing endorsement of love.

For the latter, her biological clock is ticking so now you're dealing with a woman who's laid back "play it by ear" easy going attitude is gone, and after six months she's demanding a marriage proposal because she's "tired of waiting on a man to decide when he's ready to commit". Yeah, there is nothing better than a woman who gives you a deadline to propose -_-.  It sucks, when you're the good guy. Your options can a lot of times be very small if you want the girl of your dreams; Sucks don't it?

Ok now let's talk about my favorite kind of girl. The one who isn't looking for a stereotypical "Bad Boy", or a pushover "Nice Guy" she just wants someone who she can hang out with and possibly sleep with if he doesn't say anything stupid to kill her mood. She's pretty, fun, likeable, charismatic and most of all totally head over heels for you. She understands that you have dated a few psychos and doesn't give you a hard time about little things. She realizes that you're not made of money and does not ask for a lot. She's had some bad relationship experiences but does not let the past affect the future. She's pretty much everything you would want in a girl, and I had her; her name was Zoey.

# Zoey

I think every guy has a Zoey in his life but I don't give a shit about his Zoey, I want to talk about mine. You may have noticed that I've dated a lot of good looking women, well guess what Zoey was Hawt too! Let's go over the attributes. 5'8, brown skin, light brown bedroom eyes that could look hazel on a good day, full lips, medium length brownish black hair, and a bubbly but sultry voice that you wouldn't mind hearing if you called one of those "Special" hot lines. She had an athletic build with curves. Think of the sexy sports car, but with a vagina, and you got Zoey.

I remember the day I met Zoey; it was the beginning of the second Semester of college and I pretty much barged into her room driven by hunger and the knowledge that her roommate (Natalie) always had food and was willing to share because we'll... She wanted to sleep with my roommate (God I miss college). Natalie wasn't there; instead I walked in on Zoey and her RA having a heart to heart. She skewered me with her eyes, probably because I walked into her room saying "if you feed me pop tarts I will feed you Sean's penis" Natalie would of found this funny, Zoey did not.

*um excuses me, who the hell are you?!*

The RA Tried to bail me out…. *Oh this is…..*

*I'm talking to him* *Skewers me again*

*Oh uh… Well, I must have gone to the wrong room I apologize. Do you know where I can find Natalie?*

*This is Natalie's room, I'm her roommate, and she's not here right now.*

*Oh hey, I didn't know she had a roommate now. My name is Eric nice to meet you. *offers hand shake**

**Looks at hand then continues* Eric, who told you it was ok to talk to my roommate like that?*

*Oh, well I was just joking, she knows I like to kid around with her.*

*- Well I don't appreciate that kind of talk to any of my female counterparts so please refrain from using that kind of language in my room.*

*\*Switches on charm\* ooh, I love it when you get all assertive, \*makes fake sexy face\**

*In my mind I imagined you laughing hysterically over this joke and then the ice being broken, clearly my imagination was wrong*

She gave me the slightest grin and said; *that's ok, maybe next time.*

*Oh! I see a little smile maybe not all is lost! Ok let's try this again, I'm Eric, and you are?*

*Nice rebound. I'm Zoey, Natalie's new roommate. So Eric who are you?*

After bombing miserably, Zoey and I started over and had a pretty decent conversation. I found out she was from Chicago, and wanted to be an editor for a big time magazine one day and I shared my aspirations of becoming the next green ranger. The conversation went well and I promised to try and be more respectful when coming to her room. After that we were always cordial and friendly when seeing each other. I can't say that I was head over heels because I wasn't. For the time I just thought she was a hot girl who was also really cool. But, according to my roommate (Sean) she was all I could talk about. One day while hanging out at the bookstore I found a book that gave step-by-step instructions on how to create and run your own publication. I had some money left in my book voucher account so I bought it. I had no use for the book, but I remember Zoey had mentioned she wanted to be a magazine editor and I thought she would like it.

Later that day I went to her room (Knocked first) then came in and gave her the book. She kindly accepted and that was it for at least another two weeks. Then one random Saturday night she came to my room with a message. She had just come from a party and apparently she met someone there who I knew, and wanted to let me know that they said hi. I found this strange because I didn't know anyone from the college she partied at, or anyone by the name she offered, but I thanked her for the message and on a whim invited her over to watch a movie (it was 4am).

I got to second base that night #Fistpump. The next day we had a talk. She explained that although she enjoyed our light petting session from the night before, she was not that kind of girl, and the only reason I got that far was because she was interested. Luckily for me so was I, and that my friends is how Zoey and I became an item. On a college campus this means we slept in each other's twin beds, attended events together, and shared meal card points. I would go to her room, hang out, talk, eat her snacks, and watch TV. Like most college students, I was broke during this time. But my case was really serious. Although I had a job, all of my money went to paying tuition, so there were times I wouldn't have money for simple things like laundry, food, or Netflix. Going out and hitting the town was out of the question for me. Zoey was very supportive of me, she never complained, always found ways for us to have fun without spending money and even gave me a couple of dollars here and there when I needed it. She really liked me, and didn't let the other stuff get in the way of her feelings when she could of easily gotten pretty much any guy on campus she wanted (yeah she was that pretty). Most of my stories have ended with the girl screwing me over in the end. I wish I could say this one was the same, but in hindsight I was the dirt bag that dismantled this relationship.

## And then I messed it up.

Here is a piece of advice for you lovers out there. If you're not completely over your ex, don't try to get into a relationship with someone else. I was still traumatized by past relationships, not like one particular ex-girlfriend either, I was being weighed down by an army of fucked up relationships that were destined for failure from day one. I had soundtracks for every misstep I had ever made in love, and they were blaring loud and clear in my head.

# Posttraumatic relationship disorder

You ever see one of those dogs and they were rescued from an abusive household? He's usually the sweetest thing in the world, but you must always be mindful of your actions around him because any small thing can bring him back to a high trauma moment. If this happens, the dog may react, even becoming violent. Not because he's a bad dog, it's just a reaction to a trauma that he has equipped to deal with. Well I'm the dog, and that was exactly what I did. Here is how it happened. We had a mutual (Heather) friend but I was particularly close with this friend (Who just also happened to be a girl). Heather and Zoey had a conversation, in which Zoey allegedly asked if there was something going on with Heather and I. Heather denied it because we were only friends and nothing more. That was the end of their conversation.

The following day Zoey approached me and said that someone told her that Heather and I used to date. I also denied this and when I approached Heather about the rumors, she told me that she heard Zoey was the one who started them. I instantly took this as a warning sign. Without taking out the time to talk to Zoey, I let my imagination go into overdrive, and assume all of the worst things about her. I thought back to how things started to unravel with Tricia. I noticed little white lies in her explanation, and felt myself becoming very nervous.

Zoey was a great girl, but clearly the signs were showing that she was a pathological liar. She must be cheating on me! It was at that moment that my disorder kicked in, and my traumatized thought process overpowered any kind of logical reasoning left in my mind. I vowed to distance myself from her, refusing to allow her to hurt me. This time around I would walk away before I went in too deep. I explained my plan to Heather and she agreed that this was the right thing to do.

### Read and learn

This is a step-by-step process on how to lose a girl.

**Ignore her-** After the conversation with Heather, I stopped calling Zoey, and began to visit her dorm room less frequently, when she came to see me I just wouldn't answer the door. When I did run into her I would complain about how busy I was.

**Become Flaky-** When it was too difficult to avoid her, I would make plans to hang out and then not show up. She has been the only girl who ever tried to make my birthday special, and I didn't even want to come up to her floor to see the little celebration she set up for me.

**Detach from emotions-** This is a tactic I have used frequently in my later years. But with Zoey it was the first time trying it. I slowly but surely convinced myself that she was no good for me by systematically removing any emotions I had for her. I did this by highlighting flaws, focusing on what I thought was suspect behavior, and burying myself in work to avoid any thoughts of her. The tactics worked, but Zoey didn't know what the hell was going on.

**When she confronts you-** Zoey tried to confront me to find out what the problem was. Despite everything I had done to separate myself from her she still wanted to deal with me. I avoided all verbal contact with her, and then sunk to a relationship low when I finally did end things.

## The Break up.

I finally ended things with Zoey. On a random Wednesday night I contacted her through instant messenger, and told her that things were not working out and that we should be friends. I refused to explain why I made that decision, only saying that I couldn't trust her, and that "If it looks like a duck, and sounds like a duck. It's a duck". Yeah I'm not sure what the hell I was talking about with that either. At the time of the break up I felt vindicated and free, I remember talking to my roommate at the time (Sean) and he said something to me that wouldn't register for another two years.

*Wait so you just screwed over one of the best looking girls on campus because of some shit, that another girl told you, even though you know from experience that most girls are catty, two-faced, and spread all kinds of rumors?! Wow you're a genius; you just blew it with a great girl over hearsay. Screw it, let's get drunk, it's Thursday.*

When I finally understood what Sean meant with that comment, two years had gone by and if I ever had any chance of reconciliation it was long gone.

## Hindsight is 20/20

I had a really good girl. She was pretty much everything I've said I wanted in a companion, but I failed to hold on to her because I was too immature to understand just how good I had it. I don't want to paint the picture that Zoey was perfect, because she wasn't, but no one is, and in order for any relationship to work there must be communication. I took one piece of information and used it as a reason to push away from her because I didn't want to be hurt. That's what really ended our relationship, fear. I was so screwed up from past experiences and paranoid that I would fall into the same situations that I reacted out of fear and pushed someone away who I may have been able to build something with. Maybe we would have dated for a few months and then the relationship might have fizzled out, maybe we could have dated for several years and gotten married, no one is really sure, but if I could do it over again, I would face my fears and just talk to her. I ask her for her side of the story and move on from it because my reason for pushing away was so minuscule in the larger scheme of things. There was no reason to react the way I did.

I lost that relationship because I was a coward, and when it ended I laughed because I thought she lost out on a great guy. As I close this out I can tell you there was a loser in this, but it wasn't her...

## Bitter

**Current Playlist:**

My Chemical Romance: Famous Last Words
Limp Bizkit: Behind Blue Eyes
Limp Bizkit: My Way
The Dream: Florida University
Kanye West: Street Lights

So what is the proper procedure for being hurt, bitter or feeling rejected by a girl? I know from the ruthless jokes that my friends have thrown in my direction, open dejection and melancholy is not a good idea, but I've tried the repressed feelings approached and all that accomplished was a shitty summer and ten pound weight gain. I don't have money for the strip club, and I'm not bold or good looking enough to hook up with a new girl at a bar or party. So how exactly do I get out this huge bubble of rejection, shock, embarrassment and pain? No seriously I really want to know the answer because as far as I've experienced I'm just supposed to forget my feelings and run out into the wild to fight, hunt and fuck.

Don't get me wrong, those three activities are fun as hell, but have you ever been dumped? It sucks, it really really sucks and I'm not equipped with the best techniques to handle it. And while you're at it, how do you handle a girl who plays ping pong with your emotions, would it be wrong to give her a wedgie and then push her into a crowd of people? I've had to deal with both situations, and neither has been fun. So let's discuss the latter, when a girl plays Ping-Pong with your heart.

# Kimberly

Was a Bitch... That's all you need to know, now let's get into the dialogue.. Ok, ok I'll give an introduction. Kimberly was a sandwich pick, she happened well after Tricia but way before Artimis, or Sharon. We met during my junior year of college while both being involved with student government. She was smart, quirky, quiet, and blunt, physically she was a dark skin Jamaican with a huge ass (I love big asses) shoulder length hair, a round face, big lips, and squinted suspicious eyes. I'm not sure if this description makes her look bad, but trusts me she was cute. We started working together in one of the many student government committees and after a few weeks of being in her presence I realize that I actually liked her. BIG MISTAKE!. The following is dialogue that took place during the spring college semester of 2008.

## April 25th 2008 2:15pm
Sitting in my dorm room on a brisk Saturday afternoon I decide today would be the best time to express my interest for Kimberly. So

before I can puss out I pick up my phone and dial her extension.

**Kimberly**
*Hello?*

**Me**
*Hey Kim its Eric, what's up!*

**Kimberly**
*Oh, hey Eric! No one ever calls my dorm number I thought it was the RA or something.*

**Me**
*Yeah, I'm different, I like to live on the outskirts of life.*

**Kimberly**
*Yeah.... I guess....*

**Me**
*So Kim, the reason I called is because the Anthropology club is having a movie night in the Soccer Field tonight. I was thinking we could order some food, get a blanket, and watch it together.*

**Kimberly**

*Oh! That sounds like fun, but why do you want to hang out with me during non student government hours all of a sudden.*

**Me**

*What, can't a guy just want to hang out with a girl in an intimate date like setting and it mean nothing?!....*

**Kimberly**

*No he can't*

**Me**

*I see your point, to be honest I really like you and I would love to get to know you better.*

**Kimberly**

*I'm flattered Eric but I'm not looking for a campus fling, I would be expecting something that could turn serious.*

**Me**

*That's great because so am I, I really like you.*

**Kimberly**

*Well I do think your a great guy, so let's see where this goes. But just to warn you, this won't be easy. You have to be persistent.*

## Me
*Good because I'm not looking for easy. So the soccer field is at least a 40 minute walk from the dorms, and the shuttles not running, so how about we meet at 7:15 in front of your building?!*

## Kimberly
*That's perfect, I can't wait to have our first "Date" that's what this is right?*

## Me

*Yeah it is, see you in a couple of hours.*

**Standing outside of Kim's building at 7:25pm**

**Sent to voicemail**

*Hey Kim, its Eric, I've been trying to call, but your phone keeps going straight to voicemail. I guess you're running a little late, so I'll see you in a few.*

**7:48pm Via text.**

*Hey Kim, its E. Did you forget about me? (No response)*

7:55 the RA comes on duty and lets me into the building. I go straight to Kim's floor and knock on her door. No one answers.

**April 27th 6:37pm**
I'm hanging out In the cafeteria with buddies Ross, Noah, and Brett when Kim walks up asking to talk.

We walk to a corner of the cafeteria that has no one around.

*So what the hell happened on Saturday? I was looking forward to our date all day and you just blew me off!!!!!!!*

*What?! No I didn't!!! I waited outside of your building until 8, left you two voicemails and text you three times. Then I pulled a stalker move and knocked on your door!*

*Oh... Oh \*Embarrassed laugh\* wow you did text me, and I have two unread voicemails... Ooops I guess that was my bad. Ok let me make it up to you; let's have a movie night in my dorm room. My roommate is out of town for the weekend, so we'll have some private time.*

*Yeah, that sounds great!*

*Great, I'll see you at 10 tonight, cool? Oh and bring pop corn.* She kisses me on the lips then leaves the cafeteria

## 8:00pm On the phone with Kim

*Just wanted to make sure we were still on for tonight.*

*Hey E, I can't wait to see you, I'm cleaning my room right now. Have you ever seen "The Dark Knight?!*

*Um yeah, I LOVE that movie (Batman is my favorite superhero)*

*Yeah, that's what Brett told me. We're gonna watch that tonight.*

*You just gotten a bunch of cool points! I'll see you tonight.*

10:03pm- I arrived a few minutes late to show I was in control and knock on the door.

10:04- a full minute passes by and no one answers.

10:07- three more minutes and no answer, so I send Kim a text message.

*Hey Kim I'm at your door and knocking and no one is here. I don't know if maybe you're still in the shower or something, so I'm going to run down to Brett's room on the 2nd floor for a couple of minutes then come back.*

10:20 -Back at Kim's room after taking a shot of Jack Daniels from the bottle that Brett, Ross, and Noah were drinking in his room. After knocking again the door opens and its Kim's roommate Sallie

*Hey Eric*

*Um hey Sallie*

*So what the fuck do you want?!*

*I was supposed to have a movie night with Kim.*

*Oh well, she's not here.*

*Is she in like the shower or something? I can come back in a couple of minutes*

Sallie (stares longingly into room)

*So is that what I should do?*

*Oh you're still here?! Kim went to Washington with her Tri zeta sisters, she'll be back next week.*
*What, are you sure?! I just spoke to her at like 8.*

Sallie (looking back into the room)

*Um yeah, but I'm busy can you leave?*

*Yeah I'll leave I just can't believe she blew me off like that.*

*I'm trying to give my boyfriend a blow job, can you please get of here?!*

And I left.

### April 28th 3:00am Over the Phone

*Hey Eric I'm so sorry, my sisters kidnapped me and made me come with them to DC, my battery died and I couldn't contact you.*

*Whatever have a nice life...*

*Wait no, please Eric I really like you, don't be like that. At least let me try and make it up to you.*

*Kim, you don't have to do me any favors, if you don't like me its cool, just be honest.*

*No I really do like you, just give me this last time to make it up to you. Meet me on 34th street this Friday at 8:00pm. We'll meet up, go to your favorite bar on Astor Place, get super drunk and maybe if you're lucky I'll let you get to first base.*

I contemplate this for about 8 seconds before I give an answer.

Ok I'm in but this is the last time..

**Friday May 1st. 6:30pm
(Text message)**

*Hey, I'm heading out to Penn station right now, I should be there around 7:45. Can't wait to see you!*

**7:36 (Text message)**

*Hey Kim, it looks like I got here a little early. I'm gonna hang out at the Borders on 34th and 7th, give me a call when you get here.*

**8:15 (Voicemail)**

*Hey Kim, just left you a voicemail your train must be running late give me a call.*

**8:45 (Voicemail)**

*Seriously?! I just read the "Hunger Games" from cover to cover. That book is at least 300 pages, where the hell are you?!*

**9:55 (Text)**

*Eat a Dick*

I waited another 20 minutes before I gave up and left. Two fun facts about that night. First, I was broke and purposely overdrew on my account so I could go see her. Secondly, instead of returning that money I said "Fuck it" went to the bar and got trashed out of my mind.

May 8th- My phone rings and I pick up, guess who it was?

*I know you're probably really mad at me, but I am so sorry please let me make it up to you.*

*Kim? Well yeah of course, I trust you. Listen, why don't you come to TD so we can talk things out.?*

*What's TD?*

*It will be fun and really good for you.*

*Ok cool, but what's TD?*

*TD will be a great opportunity for you why don't you just come.?*

*I want to come but what does TD stand for?!*

*It Stands for THIS DICK!*
The End........

No really, that's it.
**Next topic**

# The Motto

## Current Playlist.

John Legend "Used to love you"
Joe Budden "Where did it go wrong"
My Chemical Romance "Famous Last Words"
Slaughterhouse "Moving On"
Puddle of Mud: She Hates Me
Papa Roach: Hollywood Whore

Men are born with a certain creed... Ok maybe that's too extreme, hmmm how can I phrase this?

... Ok, men are given a few unwritten rules, I don't know who established them, I'm not sure what happened to my opportunity to vote in favor or against these rules, but they do exist. Despite what some of you female readers are thinking, the rules are actually very well known. Here are a few of them.

1. Men are tough, and don't need any emotional support
2. Men are to not express their feelings
3. Men are always supposed to be the leaders
4. Little boys shouldn't cry if they want to be Men.
5. Admitting insecurity is not allowed
6. Men must pay for all dates with women
8. Men should not ask for help
9. Men are supposed to sleep with anything with A. A pulse, B. Vagina and C. Nice tit to ass ratio. If not, said man must be drunk for penetration of mudd duck to be forgiven.

Those are just a few of them they look familiar now? Like any person there are some rules on this list that I absolutely agree with, a few I'm on the fence, and one or two where I just flat out disagree. But I didn't make the rules; I just try to follow them.

When it comes to relationships, I was always taught not to give a woman too much, don't show her that you care, outside of trying to get laid, don't show her any kind of romantic interest at all. Don't pay attention to her feelings, don't respect her or look her in the eye, because although, they say they want all of these things they become upset when you actually give it to them.

I've received this kind of instruction from older men like my father, people in my inner circle like Noah (who believe it or not is an under cover sucker for love), and my other idiot friends. They have followed these rules to the tee, and have had all sorts of success in relationships. They have all been in very happy, healthy relationships, and if they weren't in one of those they were constantly getting laid.

I have had a front row seat in seeing the man philosophy for relationships work, but for some reason I can't embrace it. I have horrible relationship habits. When the girl is talking I look her in the eye, I don't hesitate to let a girl know that I like her, when we hit a bump in the road, I like to talk it over and try to get to the root of the problem, and worst of all I really take an interest in whomever I'm seeing. Are you nauseous yet?

I know! I'm failing and I don't know how to reverse this trend, but when I'm really interested in a girl I get this unnatural urge to know everything about them, talk to them, be in their company, and try to establish something that equates to intimacy before sex. This approach has failed me almost every time but I keep right on along the same path.

What confuses me even more is that every female I know tells me that the approach I take is one that many women desire from men, but when it happens many of these said women recoil with self-destructive tactics. I would like to focus on one tactic in particular.

## Relationship Terrorism

Relationship Terrorism as defined by me is when someone in a relationship has reached a point of happiness and begins to get claustrophobic or panic. They are not used to being committed, or happy so they begin to inflict damage on their relationship in order to push their partner away. The terrorism part comes to play because their behavior is irrational, hurtful to their partner, and self-destructive for no other reason but some trumped up belief, that because you have been hurt, you must now hurt others.

 On many occasions the terrorist behavior happens because of some deeper personal issue that the terrorist has had for a while but is probably not addressing. (I.E. Daddy issues, abandonment, trust, etc).

There are always signs in the relationship that show things are not good, but they're not always evident. I wish women would hold their signs up, so I could spot them earlier. But let's get to the girl shall we? Yup there is always a girl, my life is made up of interactions with all of them.

Her name was Sharon, and she was/is a wonderful girl. We grew up in the same neighborhood, went to the same Middle School, and High School, but had not really crossed paths until long after we both graduated. I think Sharon may have been the toughest girl I've ever dated, honestly. I would never try to get into a fight with that girl. I've seen her brawl, and its not pretty. But as always I digress. She was a fair skinned British beauty with jet black hair that never stayed in one style, grey eyes that turned emerald green in the spring, a kind face with a mischievous grin... Ok so maybe she didn't have such a kind face. Did I mention that she was 5'7 with a runner's body? After high school, we lost contact until like most of my friends from the past; we found each other on Facebook. From there things were stagnant for a few months but then one day for no particular reason I wrote on her wall.

*Me- "Hey stranger! I haven't seen you since Eastern High days, I hope all is well"*

The message was short sweet and simple. A week went by before I actually got a response; I had completely forgotten I even wrote on her wall. So when Facebook was telling me that "Sharon was responding to your wall post" I didn't know what wall post she could have been responding to. I had to read my original message three times before I remembered sending it. Her response was just as simple.

*Sharon- "Heyy stranger it's been way too long, give me your number so we can catch up"*

I don't know about most people but I have a soft spot for my high school as well as the people who graduated from there. The school means a lot to me so I feel a kinship to anyone who went there. I sent her my number in a personal message. Two minutes later my Blackberry buzzed, it was a message from her.

Sharon- "Heyyy, its Sharon, save my number: -p"

I looked at the message and started smiling, in case you have not been paying attention, and know nothing about Facebook/text etiquette, when a girl sends you a message with more than one y in her "Hey" it means she wants the dick. Seriously this is a proven theory! Anyways, once I saw that "Heyy" message I knew that she was probably hot for my cock. I immediately returned her message and we went back and forth for about an hour before I made my move.

*Me- "Useless fact #1. I had a huge crush on you back in High School"*

*Sharon- "LMAO @ Useless fact... But whoa, did you really like me?"*

*Me- "Absolutely"*

*Sharon- "Wow, well why the hell didn't you ever make a move on me, I would have been very receptive"*

*Me- "Oh now you tell me lol, well I thought you were out of my league, plus there was that hole thing of me dating two lesbians by accident, one of which I told everyone I was going to marry while she was secretly sleeping with both girls and boys basketball teams"*

*Sharon- " Yeah I see your point, you did suck with the bitches"*

*Me- "Hey I don't care if you're a sorority girl, you can't haze me, but yeah you're right. 'Bitches be trippin' what can I say "*

*Sharon- " Lol, I'm not hazing you; but trust me if I was you would definitely like it" (Lusty Wink)*

*Me- "Really? Care to divulge.."*

*Sharon- " Sorry mister, I have to leave something to your imagination"*

*Me- "This is true, but you know what, why don't we meet up for some coffee, and if you don't scare me too much maybe we'll go catch a movie afterwards"*

Sharon- "hmmm is this a date request? Sounds like it, and if so I'd love to. But why go for coffee first?"

Me- "Well I suggest coffee first because if it turns out that you have completely let yourself go and gained 500 pounds since high-school I can make up a lie about having something to do and leave after the coffee is done"

Sharon- " And what if I'm still as hot, or hotter then I was in high-school?"

Me- "Whoa whoa whoa, I never said you were hot, I want to go out because I heard you were easy"

Sharon- "Oh my god I'm laughing hysterically right now, you're still the same Eric! who told you I was easy?"

Me- "I'm cool with your pimp, you know the usual people"

Sharon- "Lol, well my pimp might be wrong"

Me- "Might"

*Sharon- " Might"*

*Me- " , let's set this shit up"*

*Sharon- "Let's" (winks)*

No horn dogs, Sharon and I did not have sex that first date. We had coffee, saw a really crappy movie, and went to an open mic event in the city, then closed the night out at a bar. We definitely had the chemistry going from the minute we saw each other. Soon one date turned into two, two into three, and before you know it she was coming over to my place, and I was coming (See what I did there?).. Things were moving fast, but in a good way. She knew both of my roommates, I knew all of her friends, and she met mine, the conversations were still crisp and engaging, the sex was tip top, and things seemed to be heading in the right direction. I was beginning to think that maybe I found someone that I could build something for the long haul with. I shouldn't have been so optimistic.

# Relationship Tunnel Vision

Wondering what that is? Oh, ok I'll explain. Relationship Tunnel Vision can be explained with one word... Blindness. I'll explain further; have you ever been with someone and things were so great that you either didn't notice some of their glaring flaws, or chose to ignore them altogether? Yeah, that's what relationship tunnel vision is, when all you see is right in front of you, and not everything else that may be and usually is just as important as what is in your direct line of emotional vision. I've mastered the art of relationship tunnel vision; I try to accept everyone's flaws and all, but if you're going to be in a relationship there are some things you have to be honest with yourself about, and that includes which flaws you're willing to deal with. This is not to say that I had no flaws in this or any other relationship. I had several sissy boy behavior moments in this relationship (We'll get to that) but right now we're focusing on Sharon.

Sharon was a "Daddy's girl". This was both a good and bad thing. It was good because she didn't have Daddy issues, which as many of my lady killing friends will tell you make a girl a prime sexual partner but a relationship headache. Unfortunately, the relationship she had with her father also made every other man expendable, this included me. In her eyes, there were only two things I could give her that daddy couldn't (Penis, and head), and if I annoyed her she could either get it from someone else, or do without. She never hesitated to remind me of this. It was cute in the beginning until we got into our first argument and she dismissed me like I was a bum on the street asking for change.

The second was her demeanor. Sharon was one of those girls who had four different persona's. Her text message persona, her phone persona, her face-to-face persona, and her "social networking persona" I'll explain. Via text message she was the sweetest girl, very funny, caring affectionate and considerate, via phone call she was usually dismissive annoyed, and slightly volatile. In person, she was a combination of "Text Sharon, and Phone Sharon" I spent a lot of the relationship confused because I never really knew where I stood. Then there was her "Social Networking" Persona, but we'll get to that later.

One day Sharon and I were at my apartment, watching the Bulls game. This was nothing out of the ordinary, she and I usually spent time like this, using commercial breaks and halftime to ravage each other with quickies, and kisses, but on this occasion she didn't seem ready for one of my famous 48-second sex sprints.

*"Hold on a sex, I mean sec, hold on a second babe. I have something to tell you"*

*"Uh oh, am I in trouble? I swear I didn't mean to do it babe, Noah was the one that thought it would be a good idea to go to a strip club and throw monopoly money on the girls"*

*"You went to a strip club?!"*

*"huh?!"*

*"What?!"*

*"Nothing, so what were you saying babe?"*

*"Christoff has gotten in contact with me again"*

 Since I've never mentioned a Christophe let
me inform you; Christophe is Sharon's Ex
boyfriend, he's a blond hair blue eyed Russian
with perfect skin, and a trust fund. There are
only three things that Christophe loves:
House music, tight bright pants, and the
Boston Red Sox. Did I mention that he
cheated on Sharon with two guys at the same
time? He claims he wanted to know how anal
sex felt; she wasn't too accepting of this. I was
not a fan of Christophe because the prick
really hurt her, and I was the one left dealing
with the damage. Not my idea of fun times.
So when she mentioned that he called, my
feathers were instantly ruffled.

"What does he want?"

"He apologized for cheating on me, and wants to meet up because he's going on tour as a dj for this house group"

Are you going to see him?

"No"

"My thoughts exactly"

That was the end of the conversation, and what I thought was also the end of Christophe but now that I look back on it, that was where things took a turn.

Sharon and I both had busy schedules, but if I didn't contact her she would always contact me first, that was just the way things went. I had a particularly busy week at work and was doing a lot of running around. To say I was distracted would have been an understatement. It wasn't until that Friday that I realized we hadn't talked all week, literally not one moment of contact ALL WEEK! This struck me as weird so I called her, unfortunately my call was sent straight to voicemail. Never one to jump to conclusions I left things be for the night. I got her the next morning and my worries were at ease, for about a week. But what fun would this be if that was the end of the story?

## Social Networks and Circumstantial Evidence

You know that game we all play? Ok not everyone, maybe just the couples. You know what game I'm talking about. The one where we feel like something is off, but can't put our finger on it, and then your significant other posts a Facebook status that feeds right into what you were feeling? Well that's what Sharon did to me, CONSTANTLY! This started off on a casual Tuesday. I logged on to Facebook, and "Casually" observed the time lines on my home page (I went straight to Sharon's Facebook page to check her status updates) and when her name popped up, it's followed with this status:

["You're my little secret, and that's how we should keep it." Can't stop smiling.

This status update gives off instant red flags. What the hell does "Can't stop smiling" mean, who the hell is her little secret, and is this chick really putting something so disrespectful up on Facebook when she knows I'll see it, but most importantly, whose dick has she seen? I call her immediately to address the situation. She's annoyed that I would think she was two-timing me and explains that the status is actually lyrics, and that " if I ever paid attention to detail, I would see everything was in quotes minus the 'all smiles'.

After reviewing the status again, it was obvious that she's telling the truth. Despite the reassurance my gut instincts are in overdrive, something is definitely wrong. But with no stable ground to stand on I just looked like one of those insecure boyfriends who react with the slightest provocation. As Sharon and I spoke less frequently her Facebook "Quotes" started to multiply. Soon she was also posting "quotes" on her twitter.

Remember that thing last chapter where I mentioned her "Social Networking" persona? Well here it was. She never mentioned me on any social network, if I responded to her status, she would never get back to it, if I wrote on her wall it would get drowned out by a million other updates, if I followed her on twitter she would follow me back but then out of nowhere her timeline would be blocked from my viewing. Something was very wrong, but I still had nothing to go on. Christmas was coming around and I could feel the relationship was slipping away. I was in a panic and ready to do everything possible to salvage it. Then about a week before Christmas she gave me a call and told me she would be spending Christmas day with me. This was a very big deal because I told her on many occasions that this holiday had turned into nothing but depression central for me. She was going to spend the morning of Christmas with her family then come spend the rest of the weekend with me. She wanted a pair of super expensive boots so I did what any caring boyfriend would do. I went to the store and spent $500 dollars that I didn't have to make sure her Christmas was great, then I bought a ten dollar card and wrote her what I thought was a heartfelt Christmas message. The big day arrived and she made it to my place, ordered food and hung out for about an hour, or I hung out and she was glued to her phone texting while taking out a moment or two in order to acknowledge my existence. At 2:30 we decided to exchange gifts, I brought up her gift, which was of course the boots she wanted along with the Christmas card. She gave me her gift, a $20 dollar shirt from American Eagle, and a Christmas card from the 99 cent store (Don't laugh, I fucking love that shirt). My roommates would later laugh at me, saying that you can tell how much a girl cares about you by how much she's willing to spend, but I'm jumping the gun. We exchanged gifts, and then watched the Bulls game. As soon as the game was over she showered and left to go to a friends party in Brooklyn. My apartment was just a pit stop.

To say I was disappointed would be a lie, to say that I felt like a dick would be just about right. I've been in many relationships but never have I felt like the person I was dating did not respect me. They may hate me, they may not like me, some of them could barely tolerate me, but never has any of them ever made me feel as small and insignificant as this girl did. Christmas was spent with my roommates laughing at me for spending so much money then telling me to move on (I didn't listen).

## If she won't sleep with you...

If your girlfriend randomly declares that she no longer wants to have sex, there is something wrong. Either you suck so badly in bed she'd rather not even bother, or someone else is busting it wide open and she'd rather they become the permanent tenant in her vaginal canal. So when Sharon told me she didn't want to have sex anymore I knew for sure the relationship had pretty much disintegrated into a pile of rubble.

She sat me down and told me she didn't want to be intimate. The manly thing to do would have been to curse her out and demand even more sex than before. Instead, I said I didn't like the decision but would do my best to support her wishes. This promise on my part was followed up with her now posting status updates about being "In the mood", or "being utterly satisfied." I'm sure you know how I reacted to this... No? Ok let's get to the best part of this story.

## Passive Aggressive her

The proper term is passive aggressive, but the title better illustrates what I did to this girl. In another attempt to salvage this relationship, I broke the cardinal Man Code rule by trying to get her attention by acting irrationally. I would hear from her and give off the vibe that I was totally happy in my sexless attention less dry relationship, and then deploy suggestive status updates on twitter, openly flirt with her friends on Facebook, and go after/accept phone numbers from other women. In reality, I did all of this to get her attention, and maybe if she gave even part of a shit this strategy would have worked. But if someone does not care, you can't make him or her by doing emotional and irrational actions. I thought it would make her care, instead it seeped out whatever amount of respect she had left for me. I looked like a big whiny insecure bitch searching for hugs and reassurance.

After all of this, the relationship, or what was left of it was still going. February would be the death sentence. One of the many things that Sharon and I had/have in common is a February birthday. Mine on the 21st, hers on the 2... Don't worry about that. We agreed to hang out on Valentines day, but both birthdays were fuzzy lines because neither knew what they wanted to do yet, and this is how we get to the sledgehammer that frustrated the camel so that a straw could break its back. Sharon made it clear that all she wanted for Valentines Day was a card, chocolates and a night out at a fancy restaurant, something classy like BBQ's. I wanted to see her before V-day arrived since we hadn't hung out since Christmas. We agreed to hang out the weekend before the 14th but something happened and she didn't have the money to travel. Determined to see her, I transferred a few dollars into her account so she could travel. She never came to my place. Her excuse seemed pretty fair, she and her father had a big blow up and he forbade her from leaving her home. She still lived with him so I could very well see this happening. She texted me the details and expressed how frustrated she was. I decided to hang out with a friend from college, that friend happened to know Sharon, and throughout the weekend reported to me that Sharon via twitter spent the entire weekend partying and spending quality time with Mr. Valentine #1. Every time I texted, she would say she was home, but her twitter told me a different story. She was drunk with friends, high with friends, or happy with "Him." I was nowhere around so clearly the writing was on the wall. I closed my eyes and claimed to be illiterate; if she really were cheating I would need hard core evidence. Valentines day came and we met up. I had her chocolates, card, and candy. She had my card. Things were going well at first, I took her to the restaurant, and as per the way things had been for the last few months, the conversation was clipped. And then things took a very interesting turn. A couple walked into the restaurant and sat one table away from us. Sharon's face turned to stone. Apparently she knew the guy. When I asked she refused to admit it, but the rest of our dinner was spent with her ignoring pretty much everything I said, and trying to sneak eye contact with the guy. I took this girl out, and was spending my hard earned money on her, hadn't had sex in months, put up with disrespect and felt marginalized on more occasions than I can care to mention, and on the one day where every couple tries to at least act like they appreciate each other, she was bold enough to shit on me just a little more by spending the entire night looking at another guy. A guy she'd probably been fucking for all I knew. I quietly sat at that table, ate my sticky wings, and made a silent promise to be through with this girl. Any romantic feelings I had for her ended at that table. My blood ran cold. I couldn't wait to have her out of my sight and deleted from my memory bank. The rest of that dinner was uneventful, we ate and then I took her home. Hell bent on getting birthday sex, I asked if she was coming over for my birthday. Her response was "We'll see". I laughed it off and prepared for her to have some sort of crisis that day. Then on the big day, I got a Facebook message that say's "Babe, I lost my phone. I can't make it to your place, I'm so sorry, but I hope you have a happy birthday. I gave her a simple response: "Ok". I was actually very sick on my birthday and spent my time in bed watching the "Happy Birthday" messages on Facebook trickle in on my Facebook wall. I stopped by Sharon's page a few times, she was updating her status through a mobile phone, so much for that "lost phone" story.

The funny thing about our entire relationship is that when I finally did end things, she all of a sudden cared or at least said she cared. All of these feelings came out, she claimed to be confused as to why I felt the way I did, and had a logical explanation for everything that happened, and maybe, just maybe if she hadn't spent Valentines day looking at another guy, and then missed my birthday all together, I might have been able to look at her side of things and try again. But as I said before, my blood had run cold and I didn't want anything else to do with her. We ended things on good terms, agreeing to delete each other as Facebook friends because it was

"Too painful" to see the other in any way even if it was just a status update. When it was all said and done, I wasn't sad, upset, or even reflective; as far as I was concerned I did everything in my power to make her love me. But as I learn time and time again, you can't make someone feel something that's not there.

# Hindsight is 20/20

I dated a girl who did not respect me, that was my first mistake, but instead of leaving her or demanding respect I stayed and tried to make things work. When I suspected something was wrong I still stayed and ignored the piling warning signs, so although I feel wholeheartedly that Sharon's approach to me was fucked up, I really have no one to blame but myself. No one held a gun to my head; I stuck it out because I thought things would change. It's taught me to be honest with the women in my life. As things deteriorated, I became even more irrational and tried to manipulate her emotions through calculated actions. This was self-destructive and I dropped the ball by even trying to use it. I'll never really know what happened between Sharon and me but at this point I don't care.

## How I almost gave up.
**Current Playlist:**
Eminem: Love The Way You Lie
B.O.B. Ghost in the Machine
Eminem: Space bound
Papa Roach: Forever
Wale: The War
Wale: The Breakup


There was a time where I almost gave up, not on life I'm not that much of a bitch. But there was a moment, and to be quite honest there was a couple of seconds, minutes, hours, days, weeks, and months, where I felt like maybe the way I had been living was wrong. Maybe I shouldn't be so open about letting people into my life, maybe I do get attached too fast, maybe I do go after the wrong girls, and maybe I trust the wrong people. After years of experiences with people, places, friends, hundreds of relationships, some personal, some intimate, some professional I finally doubted my approach to life. It was a moment that I will never forget, a feeling that I can't duplicate a tragedy, triumph, and coming of age all crammed into one experience. But before we talk about my stage ten Emo crisis it's rather important that we discuss the unwritten rules of relationships ending etiquette.

## How to Dump Someone.

1. Be Honest, but not cruel
2. Be upfront
3. Don't stall it
4. Don't go back on your word
5. Mean it

## How Not to Dump Someone.

1. Cut off all communication without saying a word
2. Cheat on them
3. Over Instant messenger, Twitter or Facebook
4. With a Birthday Cake
5. Don't be a dick.

The rules for ending a relationship are not overly complicated. It more or less comes down to that one cardinal rule "Don't be a dick". The person you're dating may be the worst person ever to walk this earth, they may very well deserve every single evil thing you have wished on them, but that still does not give you the right to be a dick. Breakups happen every day, but one of the hardest breakups to get past is the one where the person who dumped you is a complete dick. No one like's dealing with a dick, and if you do… well I hate you because that's just stupid.

In order to properly explain how someone could be considered a "Dick" when breaking up with their significant other, consider the following.

A couple of two years are in an argument, Partner A is mad at Partner B because she found out that he cheated on her. Partner A and B argue for several hours but Partner B is finally able to persuade Partner A to forgive him. They consummate this with makeup sex.

When the sex is over, Partner A must leave to go to work, when Partner B say's

"I know I said I wanted us to stay together, but I think I'm good now; so we're still broken up"

**DICK MOVE**

If I must explain to you where the Dick Move took place, or why this is considered a Dick Move, you're more than likely a DICK.

### Exhibit B

You have been with your boyfriend for three years, things aren't working out and you want to end things. On the night you plan to do it, something happens and he ends up in the hospital. While he's in the hospital you cheat on him with one of the guys that put him there. He finds out about the relationship on twitter.

**DICK MOVE**

Being a dick is easy, having some vagina (Balls are weak, vagina's can take a pounding) and doing the right thing is a lot harder. But when you end things the right way you do yourself and that person a valuable favor.

## Almost Post Grad.

My College days were officially numbered. No really, I literally had four days as a college student left. After spending five years in ignoring my weight and gaining an amazing freshman, sophomore, junior, and then senior 15 pounds and weeks of prodding from Brett, I finally decided to start going to the gym. Ok I won't lie; Brett tricked me into going, by promising a bottle of Jack Daniels at my door for my last night as a college student. This promise was made in the first week of my last semester; I was going to the gym 3 times a week religiously with Brett as my personal trainer. With his help, I actually lost a lot of weight and was finally starting to resemble the dashing young man that left Brooklyn for the college life. Brett and I always shot the shit between sets, and of course our favorite topics were women. I constantly had women troubles, and he was currently in a happy relationship. So four days before my college career ended, Brett and I hit the weight room, and started discussing my dismal love life.

- *"Bro you're always trying to kiss these girls in the mouth"*

*"That's not true, I don't always kiss mouth, sometimes I'm just trying to get some ass"*

- *"You're not built for that kind of life, you're the type of dude that would kiss a girl in the rain with your eyes closed while "I want it that way" played in the background*

*" But you can't lie, that is a great song?!"*

*"Great American Classic", but seriously you go after all of the wrong girls, and then when you get them, you're way too nice. See a guy like me, I just be like, ' Ay come get dis dick right here' girls like that rough ignorant shit"*

*Any female that would fall for that is the type of woman that I would never want to date bro.*

*Who said anything about dating?! We're in our 20's you should be fucking everything in sight. You should be training your penis, I'm trying to save your marriage,*

*But since you want to go in that direction I have somebody in mind, Artimis...*

*Artimis... Oh her?! Isn't she crazy?*

*No, she's not crazy.... Just passionate*

*Once I hit her with the, charm and flash these 3 pack abs, she's going to be down for the swirl.*

She was NOT down for the swirl. Give me a minute and I'll explain what happened, but first let's introduce this lovely lady.

# Artimis

Artimis for lack of better words is a professional asshole. It's one of the things I love about her! I remember she begged me to watch one of the twilight movies (New Moon) and when I finally relented, and actually enjoyed it she called me a "Bitch" for not standing my ground. This girl has such a smart mouth, and if you can't take a joke you really shouldn't hang out or have any conversation with her because it's almost guaranteed she will say something that will either confuse or rub you the wrong way. I spent countless evenings quietly laughing at the way people would react to her dry humor and snarky comments. She was my little asshole (Actually that sounds kind of weird). But don't let the sarcasm fool you, she "tries" to come across as someone who doesn't really care, but I like to believe that I can read through her bullshit. When her guard is down she's the kind of person that people just gravitate towards. She can walk into a room full of strangers and before the night is over she's exchanging stories and inside jokes like they've been best friends for as long as either can remember. But if you ask her she'll say she hated every moment of the interaction, does not know or understand what people see in her and would have rather been left to her own devices.

This is a girl who swears to every God that she hates people, but anyone who has ever gotten to know her falls in love.

She's, 5'7, with daisy yellow skin, black curly hair that goes down to her back, a long nose, and bright attentive eyes. She played basketball in high school, and still goes to the gym from time to time to school people, but has a body built for a model.

I sent her a message on Facebook shortly after my conversation with Brett. I wanted to express my interest without coming on too strong, and after 6 minutes of hard thinking, I settled for the following message.

"Hey what's up, I know we haven't really spoken before but I've seen you on campus and thought you were cool. I would love for us to hang out some time. Maybe alcohol or something, what do you think?"

Her response went something like this:

*" First of all I don't know you, so why are you contacting me on Facebook. Clearly you are some kind of sick stalker. Secondly I dated your friend Brett and I don't know what he told you but I'm not just some slut you can pass around, so I don't appreciate you hitting me up thinking you're going to get something, you're ugly, I don't want you and your breath stinks.... P.S. You're a bitch for writing me on Facebook"*

I responded to her initial message addressing some of her grievances explaining that I heard nothing bad at her. And closing out my response with the following:

-No one can resist my charm so she eventually responded.
 *For the record, it should be known that I am dead sexy, and eat breath mints every day, so you're just a hater.*

*"Well whatever, I don't like you and I never will. You're still a bitch for trying to hook up with me on Facebook, but I guess I'm sorry for freaking out on you without knowing what you were really about"*

We didn't speak for a couple of months, in between this time I graduated from college, got my first real job, dated Sharon, found my back bone, and started working on my first book. When things were slow at work I would get on twitter post comments on whatever came to mind. For some reason people found me hilarious, and before you knew it I had a bunch of followers, guess who one of them was?! Yup you guessed right if you said Artimis. She followed me so I gave her a follow back. Over the next couple of weeks via twitter we learned that we had a lot of things in common.. This revelation helped to soften her shell and eventually we exchanged phone numbers and scheduled a date.

## We hit it off

No really, we hit it off, and hard. I swear if
you would have looked over my phone bill at
the time, 80% of my phone calls and text
messages were to her. We would talk all day
about anything. Sometimes we agreed,
sometimes we didn't, but the conversations
always rolled along. I loved talking to her
because we could be on the phone all night
and it would feel like minutes, this did suck
when we had things to do because we would
plan to only speak for five or six minutes and
by the time the conversation had run its
course 3 hours whirled by and neither person
would have an explanation for how that much
time passed with no one noticing. Our first
date does no justice in explaining our bond; I
think we were both just trying to see what it
was. The following dates are when we really
started to grow into each other.

Dating Artimis was like hanging out with a
best friend whose brains I wanted to fuck
senseless. We hung out, talked with the ease

that does not usually happen with people dating, and did I mention that we both wanted to bang each other senseless? Oh and she was crazy about me! No really she was. I've mastered the art of dating women who I seem to like more than they would like me, but for once I had done things right. I've always gone by the motto of if a woman really cares for you, it's evident in her actions. In all of my years of dating I had never seen a woman look at me the way she did. It was a combination of adoration, disbelief, and relief. We'd be having a conversation and she would just look at me like I wasn't real, then of course would catch herself and punch me in the arm and tell me to "Stop being a bitch" but she wasn't slick, I knew exactly what that look meant. She opened up by telling me things that she would not dare mention to another soul. I was her escape from the ugliness of the world, creating our own little universe where we were the only people allowed. Nothing else mattered when she was around. In a crowded room it was just me and her. When my first apartment flooded and destroyed pretty much everything I owned, she was the one that helped me move what was left of my possessions to my dad's house, then drove all around queens to help me find as she put it, " a decent air bed for your bitch ass to sleep on until you can find an apartment and a bed et I might consider letting you fuck me on". And when I was apartment hunting and refusing to eat anything in my dad's house (that's another story) she made sure I had something to eat and listened to me vent over feeling like a second-class citizen in my parents house. Our chemistry was crazy. We would kiss and I would get that drunk feeling that people are always mentioning in those shitty romantic novels. Were we falling in love? Yup I'm a hundred percent sure we were, either that or someone put a molly in my drink.

We weren't together for a very long time, but things were progressing nicely, we still had a lot of fun together, were going on dates, and started transitioning from really "Liking each other" to wanting to build a relationship that could last.

And then one day she sent me a text message early in the morning. She didn't want to take our relationship any further. In an earlier conversation she mentioned that she would push people away when she felt herself getting too close to them, she had a really unhealthy relationship with her first love and it scarred her so much that she vowed to never get that close to a man again. But I wouldn't let her end things. I fought with her for three days; it was always very obvious when we fought. All you had to do was check her or my twitter timeline, and read the bickering in our mentions; this went on for three days. 72 hours of hostile phone calls, tweets, text messages and voicemails. One of the things I learned during this time was that she could be very cold when she felt the need arise. But eventually I thawed her out and she rescinded, admitting that she did want to be with me but was afraid of being hurt.

There will come a time in your life where you meet someone and everything about the way you feel for them feels right, it felt good so I went with it; In a lot of ways, it was overwhelming because any time I've ever developed very strong feelings for someone, things end up going downhill, but my feelings for her were so different, intense and tender, composed but giddy. It was a combination of every good feeling I've ever had over any girl multiplied by ten, so I decided that although I was taking a risk, it was a risk worth taking.

Every other relationship that I've been in has had warning signs. Things that I should have picked up on, a conversation I took too lightly, If there were signs in this one. I didn't see them. I was completely blindsided. One day while talking on the phone, Artimis mood changed and she said she had something to tell me.

*I want you to meet my friends.*

*Ok cool, when?*

*Lets go to that water park in jersey.*

And that's what we did. She with her three best friends and I with one of my Fraternity Brothers (Rick) embarked on a trip to wet roller. A water park located in New Jersey, admittedly Rick and I had been drinking obnoxiously the night before and were a little hung over, but not enough to kill the mood.

The day went pretty well actually, we got on a million rides, snuck beer into the park and got drunk on a boat ride, then shared a group dinner filled with conversation. At the end of the night Rick and I headed to my Apartment while Artimis headed home with her friends. She called me when she got home that night to let me know she made it back in one piece and would talk to me the next day.

I didn't hear from her the following day, but that wasn't too weird. She might be busy, and then three days went by without me hearing a word. I sent her a text message to see if things were ok, but didn't get a response. The next day I texted again and got no response so I decided to call her, the phone kept going to voicemail. I called two more times after that and left a voicemail but once again I didn't get a response. I logged on twitter and sure enough she was there talking her usual smack and offering social commentary. I sent her a message there and she responded by blocking me.

Now I was really confused, I tried calling again and now her phone said she wasn't receiving calls from my line anymore. I tried to go on Facebook but she blocked me from posting on her wall. She went as far as cutting off communication with people who she thought I would be friends with.

I had no idea what was going on and no one would give me answers, she was ending our relationship and I hadn't gotten the heads up.

## High Fidelity Symptoms

Remember in that awesome movie "High Fidelity" when the main character finds out that his ex girlfriend is sleeping with their neighbor? Yeah it was that bad and then some. I was definitely hurt over what happened with Artimis and I, but life had to go on, I had work and other such things to handle, but she was always on my mind. One of my favorite times of this era (NOT) was when I would be living my life peacefully, and just when I thought I was finally getting over the entire ordeal the image of Artimis randomly popped up in my head.

# Super Awesome Mental Images

Now for most people, this would happen when they finally had some alone time for bad thoughts to surface, but not I. I would be in important meetings at work, or on a crowded train heading home and that vivid image would just materialize into my head coaxing all kinds of suppressed anger. I quickly learned that if I buried myself in work and didn't think about it I would be ok. But my mind wouldn't allow me, so I'd be in the middle of a meeting when the image of Artimis would pop into my mind. She would usually be in the wheelbarrow position on my bed (that never actually happened.)  My imagination is just an asshole) which would then cause me to involuntarily utter one of three phrases "Fuck" "Inaudible growl" "what the shit" I actually uttered that last phrase while on a phone conference meeting with my boss.

Yeah, it almost never went well when I had those outbursts, and that guy was a grade a douchebag. Funny story about him, he ended up getting arrested for being caught masturbating on a roller coaster am I the only one who finds that wired?

There is another part in that movie (High Fidelity) where the main character goes outside in the rain and calls out to his ex from right below her window. It's possibly one of the most pitiful examples of heartbreak I've ever witnessed, but the shit was real. I managed to emulate that pitiful heartbreak behavior as well. Here's a quick highlight reel.

*8:01pm (Voicemail) Artimis, Babe, I need to understand. Why did you do this, I thought we were doing so well, I'm not mad I just want answers. We can work this out!*

*8:03pm (Voice Mail)- Slut! How could you do this, did you suck his dirty dick?! I heard he had crabs, I hope you got crabs from his dirty dick that you probably sucked!*

*8:07pm (voicemail)- Hey I'm sorry about the message from earlier, I was just really upset. I don't know how to handle this; can we just talk?*

*8:10pm (Voicemail)- Why do you keep sending me to voicemail?! Stop being a coward and talk to me!*

*Text messages*

*2:04am (text)- I miss you*

*2:26am (text)- Don't you even miss me a little?*

*7:00am (text)- Sorry about the text from last night, I was drunk.*

*Artimis (text)- Its ok I understand.*

*Me to Artimis (Text)- So can we talk?*

My Phone's text inbox- empty.

I didn't stop calling or texting Artimis, I would call or text every single day. I never got a response but I couldn't stop. I started off trying to figure out what was wrong with her, but after weeks of ignoring my messages my emotions eventually shifted and I needed to know what had gone wrong. She finally responded.

*Are you dumb deaf or blind?! I don't want you?! I don't want to talk to you or see you, we have nothing to discuss so just leave me alone, stop stalking me! Oh and I have a date with a good friend of yours, have fun knowing he'll be rounding third base while you're at home beating your dick.*

I read her message four times, I never thought that my behavior could be considered stalker like. And "Beating my dick", what was wrong with this chic?! My masturbation was artful love making. All I wanted were answers; I needed to know what happened so I could understand how things could have gone so wrong. Until her disappearance the relationship was doing great, what could have happened so fast to change her mind about me?! My confidence was shattered, I felt ugly and stupid, I imagined her hanging out with her friends laughing at all of the heartfelt texts I sent her. I was so depressed I couldn't even sleep. I kept imagining her pointing and laughing. I started to think that something was wrong with me, maybe I was flawed, and maybe I deserved this kind of treatment. There is nothing like a painful breakup to make you reflect on past relationships. I never realized how hurtful my actions could be until someone decided it was appropriate to break my heart with a reinforced sledgehammer.

I've probably said it before, but this one hurt the most, it made the least sense and it left me looking for answers that no one was able to give. I made an entire Album compiled with songs added to help me make sense of what happened. Eminem's "Love the way you Lie" Def Leopard "Love Bites" B.O.B's "Ghost in The Machine" were my top three, but trust me there were more. This was as bad as it had ever been, and had it not been for my iPod who knows where I would be.

I consider myself to be a strong guy, but I don't know how anyone could go through this kind of pain. And if you have ever put someone else through this, I can't understand how you could ever be so heartless, to knowingly manipulate someone and then make every effort to ignore them and dismiss their emotions. If you can do this to someone and feel no pain then I want nothing to do with you.

I continued to torture myself. I should have deleted her from Facebook, but I didn't; so I was rewarded with multiple pictures of her enjoying random guys like they were sampling flavors at cold stone

## How did I get over it

That's a good question, and to be honest I don't know if I ever did. It wasn't one of those break ups you could just walk away from, you left this knowing for sure that a piece of you was forever gone. A healthy relationship ends with both partners at least knowing its over. When you think everything is going peachy only to find that the rug has been pulled from underneath your feet. How do you recover from being shot in the heart by the person you trusted the most?

I didn't get closure, I didn't understand. But from what I'm told, men don't get attached, so all I had to do was get between a new set of legs and I would feel better. So I played my role as the unfeeling man and fucked until the pain disappeared.

I wonder if she felt it too, did she ever miss our conversation, the way we always had something in common, that peaceful feeling we felt when it was just us. I wondered if she could hear my heart breaking when we ended things, and whether that affected her. I wonder if what I had with her was real. I guess I'll never know.

**Long Distance Relationships Are Bad!!**
**Current Playlist:**
Jay Z Feat Kanye West- Lift Off
B.O.B. Lovelier Than You
Wale: The Breakup

Actually they're not. Or they don't have to be. The decision is really dependent on you and your partner. Generally people usually don't begin their relationships across state lines. It's not impossible to have a relationship with someone who's not there, it's just very inconvenient, lonely, and just well… kind of stupid. More than likely, a relationship turns into a long distance one when a partner moves away because of school, work, family, or the witness protection program (That doesn't really happen right?). When one of these situations occurs you meet with your partner and one of three things happen. You break up, you go on an extended break (Breaking up), or the two of you decide that for some reason, you can defeat all odds and that your love is stronger than anything else including miles of distance. So you decide to maintain a long distance relationship.

For those of you who have never had the pleasure of being in one of these, I'll start off with the good things that can come out of this kind of relationship… NOTHING. Ok I'm lying. If you're serious about the person you're dating having one of these relationships could possibly be one of the best things that happens to you and here is why

1.    **You're forced to really get to know each other.** When you're partner is easily accessible at all times, it's harder for you to get a chance to miss them. For most couples, the hardest part about spending time together is finding the free time. Once you have that it's just a matter of getting to your partner's place, them getting to yours, or meeting up to go out somewhere. If your partner is in another state, that luxury is now gone. Your quality time is relegated to video chatting, text messages, and phone calls that must be scheduled in to fit both of your hectic days. If you're lucky and the state that they moved to is a decent drive away, maybe you see each other on the weekends, but that's a big maybe. If they aren't within driving distance, prepare

to rack up on flyer miles because you will be spending a lot of money on plane tickets. But wait, don't get depressed. If you have a strong relationship, the distance will help you become better at communicating; you learn more about someone when all you can really do is listen to what they have to say. When they're not around as much, you have more of an opportunity to appreciate all of the good things that they do, and maybe the little things that the two of you shared in a relationship. When you do reunite for good, the bond will be stronger than ever.

**2.     Harder to become reliant on your partner.-** Couples are notorious for spending so much time together that their friends begin to forget where one person ends and the other begins. They don't mean for this to happen. But when you're spending a lot of time with someone on a constant basis, it only makes sense that you begin to pick up on some of their habits. And if you're not picking up on their habits, some couples spend so much time together, that they begin to ignore everyone else. This as we should all know is a bad idea, because no matter how awesome any particular relationship is it is important to have your own friends, hobbies, personal space, etc. This is important for many reasons, but above all else your sanity. When you're with someone who lives hundreds or thousands of miles away, you're forced to get a life outside of that relationship. Your partner isn't around and it would just be sad to sit around all day waiting for their call or text. So instead you fight to make the relationship work, but you have other things going on in your life as well. It could be a hobby, obsession, friend or even a habit. But it's something other than your partner. If things don't work out you have something else going for you. A long distance relationship that works is one where the partners want to be with each other, but they won't die from not being able to be around each other as much as they used to.

Those were my two reasons, and if you think it was easy to come up with legitimate reasons of how Long Distance relationships can be a good thing; you are a jackass. Now that we have handled the pros, we can get to the easier part, the cons!

·      **Out of sight can a lot of times mean out of mind-** While for some people absence can make the heart grow fonder, in the reality of others when someone goes from making constant appearances in your life, to being relegated to how strong your internet connection is, it can be a lot easier to forget about them. Some couples try the long distance thing not realizing just how important it is to see and be with their partner. It can be very hard to be faithful to a person who isn't even under the same state lines as you.

·      **No Sex-** This one goes off of the assumption that you were sexually active before distance became a factor. If you plan on being exclusive there are going to be lots of cold, lonely, sexless, nights, afternoons, days, and evenings. You might not think it's a big deal, but for some, it is one of the most important parts of a relationship.

·      **The Unknown-** There is nothing worse than the unknown. Just imagine one of those nights where the inevitable argument comes up, the relationship is struggling under the pressure from the distance and you don't know how much longer things will continue to last going this way, what's to keep your partner from cheating? That is just one unknown variable that can come up in a long distance relationship, and trust me there are more.

There are a lot of other things that make these kinds of relationships difficult, but either they have something to do with the three listed, or I'll get into it later.

**Sex, Relationships, And What Not**

I've taken a lot of bumps, some have been unavoidable, and others were of my own making. After what felt like a lifetime of horrible experiences, I sort of got to a point where I was mentally burnt out. Sharon and Artimis left me emotionally tapped and my attitude had a shift. Artimis came back into the picture, and we tried to make the relationship work again. Things went well for about a week before she completely cut off all communication. No call, text, email, Facebook message, or explanation. It was then that I gave up on the notion of love or finding "The One" and over a six month period I became one of the assholes that I heard so many women complain about. Things got really bad, at one point I slept with at least ten different women in a month. My friends loved this "New Me". There was a new face coming into my apartment every night, my phone was always going off, and it was becoming very clear that I had a knack for not only talking to women, but getting them into bed. Everyone was happy, and I mean EVERYONE.. Well except for me. There is a funny thing about having multiple partners. The sex might be great in the moment, but when it's done, there's this hollow feeling. You look over at this person you were just intimate with, and all you seem to want is for them to leave. They have served their purpose and really they can offer you nothing else. In the beginning that feeling was ok. I was still hurting and to be frank, I didn't care how I made anyone else feel. My only goal was to bury all of my frustrations, failures, and heartache into whatever girl made it to my bedroom that night. I used these women to fill a void, but that void was like a cup with a hole at the bottom. No matter what I put into it, in the end it would always be empty.

My whorish ways had to come to an end eventually, and they did, with a bang… Literally, my last sexual partner during that six month tear was the one that finally woke me up. She was a girl who to be honest, I wasn't really interested in. We were out with a bunch of friends in the city, and it was too late for her to travel home so I told her she could crash at my place. When we got to my house I tried to go to sleep, but she had other plans in mind. For the first couple of minutes I just ignored her, but through some very suggestive encouragement tactics she got my attention (All pun intended). I could have turned her down; instead I followed the man code: "Never turn down an easy lay". We had sex, I wasn't into it or her but we did it. When we were done she fell asleep, but I was wide-awake and thoroughly disgusted with myself. I didn't fall asleep at all, instead I spent the night laying on my back recounting the past six months and trying to figure out what had happened to me. That morning I woke her up with a bowl of cereal and some money for a cab. She wasn't too happy about being rushed out, especially since she wanted to go another round, but she left. I promised myself that I wouldn't have sex again unless I was either in a committed relationship, or that the girl and I were headed in that direction.

# Eva

After six months strong of complete whoring, my new found celibacy was refreshing. I was becoming a slave of sex, and forcing myself to take a step back was probably one of the smartest decision I have ever made. I became more productive, started getting involved in my community, and was going to the gym more ( What a surprise). Now that sex wasn't running my life, I could do things like find a new job. After sending out a million applications, I was contacted by a group based in Colorado, they wanted to fly me in for an interview. Brett fell in love, got married and moved out there with his wife, I decided to turn it into a weeklong stay.  I spent my first day interviewing for a job that I eventually turned down, and the rest of the week hanging out with Brett and his wife Artimis… Just kidding, he married a girl from back home named Jenny. Jenny has been in and out of Brett's life for quite some time, so she's pretty familiar with my relationship struggles, and had someone she wanted me to meet.

*"Eric, I know you're only here for a few days, but I want you to meet my girlfriend Eva"*

*"Brett, you didn't tell me your wife was bi"*

*"You know what I mean jerk, now stop acting silly before I tell her not to come. She's a sweetheart and reminds me of the female version of you."*

*"I'm not really looking to find a love connection"*

*"Don't worry about all of that, just trust me. You will love her!"*

Jenny was right, I did love her. Eva was a beauty; standing at 5'7 she had a honey complexion with brown eyes, long black shoulder length hair, full but soft lifts, and soft features. She was soft spoken, and mellow, but also very intelligent and oozing with sarcasm (I love Sarcasm). We took to each other right away and I spent the rest of my time in Colorado with her. I left unable to get her out of my mind. From there we would talk every day. She was such an interesting character, and really unlike any woman I had ever dealt with. I never met someone who could make everything sound soft and sweet. She could be completely pissed at me and have all sorts of vulgarities flying from her mouth, but it would sound like the sweetest thing in the world. I'm not quite sure when we decided that we were going to be a couple. It wasn't one of those things that either one of us discussed. All I know is one day she and I were on the phone, and I realized that I didn't want her to be with anyone but me. Luckily she felt the same. Long distant relationships are hard, but when you start off from day one dealing with distance, the odds of it succeeding are slim to none. But we were betting against the odds.

In the beginning our relationship flourished with the distance, we couldn't see each other at all. I lived In New York, and she in Colorado, the first six months of our existence as a couple were spent on Ovoo, Skype, IPhone, Face time, Facebook chat, text messaging and late night phone calls. We talked every day and the conversation never got old. We talked about our dreams, goals, pet peeves, intentions, and of course the everyday job of existing. No matter how busy either of our schedules got we always made time to speak to each other, but most important of all we had a plan. The relationship was only supposed to be this way for a year. I would take that time to look for work in Colorado, and eventually move out there. Her entire family was out there, and leaving my home state didn't scare me. I saw going to Colorado as a new opportunity, the economy didn't seem to agree with me.

I was sending out 5-6 applications a day, but no matter how qualified I was, or interested the company seemed, I still had not found a situation which would have allowed me to feel comfortable in moving out there. Eva wanted me to take a job at a call center and worry about finding a job in my career when I got out there. But I spent four years in college for a reason, and refused to take a job I felt was beneath what I deserved. The year had flown by and I still hadn't found a job.

**If you want to hear the Base God laugh, tell him your plans.**

With our plan falling apart, things started to get a little rough. Eva was trying to be patient, but realistically how long can you sit and wait for someone before you begin to get impatient. The following things occurred:

1.     **Questioning**- Eva began to question my level of commitment to this relationship. How could she trust that I was all in on us, if I wouldn't even compromise a little bit and take a smaller role to move out there? As the days progressed where I wasn't finding work, she began to be less confident that I would ever make it out there.

2.     **Frustration**- Sexual frustration that is. Eva was going two years straight without sex. She admittedly began to flirt more often with the men around her. Maybe she didn't do anything with these guys, but she definitely had a flirtier streak to her. I was in New York dealing with the same level of frustration, and also finding it a lot harder not to take up the offers from some of my past ventures.

3.   **Passiveness**- In the middle of July I told her that I was coming for a visit, unfortunately for me I had said this on three or four other occasions and was forced to cancel because of work related issues. So when I said it that time she didn't believe me. I even sent her a picture of my plane ticket and her only response was "We'll see".

Unlike the previous times, I did actually make it to Colorado. Our reunion was a bit awkward, but after spending some quality time together we started to get back to how things were. By the time I left our relationship was energized and we were ready to really make a push. Or so I thought.

## Long Distance relationships are Hard

I'm sure I've said this couple of times, but they really are. If you're going to get into a relationship like this, more than anything you need to be 100% honest with yourself. I don't think Eva and I were. As much as I wanted to be with her, my career was, and still is the most important thing in my life. I will do anything necessary to accomplish my goals. New York is the best place for the kind of work I was trying to do, Colorado is great but the market just isn't there. So unless something drastically changed, I would never find the kind of work I was looking for. Eva was comfortable in Colorado, she had a great job, a huge condo, and her entire world was out there. It made no sense for her to leave a place where she was deeply established to try and start over in New York. We started speaking less; it seemed that someone was always busy. There was less time for casual conversations and the text messages became forced. Before I knew it she and I would go two or three days without saying a word to each other.  She started to make new friends.

There was one guy in particular whom I was definitely leery of. She would go on my Facebook page and see all kinds of suggestive comments on my wall. When she asked me about it I would brush her off and tell her not to worry about it, but then my profile pic would be of me and some random girl,(Yeah I was dumb). No relationship can work if you don't have communication and trust. Those two things are even more important when your partner is across several state lines. Things were going downhill fast. She and I were barely speaking, and suspicion of infidelity was ringing from both sides.
I knew the relationship was over, but I'm selfish. I figured if I just acted like we were fine and didn't acknowledge the obvious, things would go back to the way they once were. Eva is far too intelligent to think like that.

*"We have to address the fact that we barely speak anymore"*
*"I know, but we both have busy schedules, I don't take it personally"*

*"Eric you know its more than that. I miss the way things used to be, I miss you"*

*"I miss you too. I don't even understand how things got this weird, we were doing so well and now, I just don't know"*

*"Are you seeing anyone out there in New York?"*

*"No, absolutely not… but there is a girl out here who, I don't know; I think she's interesting"*

*" Don't worry, I know how you feel. There's a guy out here who's from New York, he and I talk every day, I feel like I'm using him as a substitute for you. That's not good."*

*"Yeah I know, so where do we go from here Eve?"*

We ended our relationship that day. After a little over a year of trying to make it work, we both finally came to terms with reality.

## Hindsight is 20/20

In a perfect world, Eva and I might still be together, but if it were a perfect world we would live in the same state and have been able to have a relationship that could either become something great, or run its course. The world is not perfect so I'm in New York, and now she's in Texas (She moved). Some people might read this and think that we were both crazy for even bothering, or they'll look at my previous history and assume that I was in a relationship with myself while Eva ran around Colorado getting plowed. I like to believe, that this time things were different. Actually I know things were different this time. And if they weren't well I guess that's just my luck. I learned a lot about women, but I learned even more about myself. What I need from my partner, what I can bring to the table, and how to communicate. Eva gave me something that a lot of the women I dated never could, a friend. We were best friends, she knows more about my life than any other person. More than Noah, Brett, Chris, or anyone else in my circle of friends, she was my pillar of strength and my listening ear. And when I got lazy, she was the one to kick me in the butt and keep me honest. Every woman after her has to bring that to the table, and because she gave it so easily I now knew that such a thing was possible. It empowered me; there was never a reason to settle for less. Since Eva and I couldn't see each other all of the time, I got better at reading emotions, and listening for the unspoken phrases. I'm a lot better at catching a hint. The friend zone was still an enemy but I was better at being clear with what I wanted from someone, and if the girl and I were not on the same page I was no longer afraid to walk away. Who knows, maybe someday she and I will have a fair shot, maybe not. Either way I'm grateful for our time together.

**To Sum It All Up**
**Current Playlist:**
B.O.B. Lovelier Than You
Journey: Don't Stop Believing

I have this problem; I'm sure after reading this book many of you will say I have SEVERAL. But I'd just like to talk about one, its really nothing more than an idea to be honest, but this idea has been the catalyst to many of my relationship choices. Ok ready for it? Here it goes; I honestly believe that there is a perfect match for every single man and woman in this world. I'll explain. I once heard this story, and since I don't remember it word for word you should accept this paraphrase of it as is. The story said that in the beginning of time all humans were physically connected. We all had four hands four legs and two heads; to put it simply two people were connected to one body. And it was during this time that we were happiest, because our days were spent laughing and playing; there were no worries. The Gods saw this and became jealous that we spent so much time intertwined with each other and not worshipping them, so they cut us in half out of spite and from that day on every man and woman spends a good portion of their life trying to find their "other half." Some of us are able to recognize them right away, many go through several partners, and although, its nice its not the perfect match and like a puzzle, if its even slightly off it just won't fit, not for long anyway. Some of us try to settle for whatever is closest to perfect and they're content, but just like a real puzzle will never be complete until you put it together in the proper places. We will never be completely whole until we find the person that belongs to us. Humans have become terribly jaded and this concept is one that many will laugh at, but I know in my mind that it is true. There really is that one perfect person out there for everyone, you just have to be willing to look for and find him or her. That's why I could never hate Clara, Tricia, or Artimis. Things ended very painfully. But if you have never been in love let me be the first to tell you its one of the greatest experiences in the world. So maybe those three weren't meant for me, but if nothing else they bring me one step closer to finding that right one. If what I had with them was just a flash in the pan, imagine what will happen when I find the right one? And sure maybe I'll try and fail with a lot more girls in the future, but the beauty of this is that I only need to be right once, I'll take the leap of faith 200 times, crash and burn 199 times, and that one time I don't it means I'm flying!

And yes, maybe I am in love with the concept of love, but what's wrong with that? Love plays such a big part of our lives, why wouldn't I? This book doesn't even begin to tell of my struggles, and it probably won't see my triumph but if another girl breaks my heart and another friend laughs at me for trying so hard it won't change who I am today, yesterday or who I plan to be forever: The Ultimate Sucker For Love. I hope my future wife can handle it.